: DUE

HOW I SURVIVED MIDDLE SCHOOL

Into the Woods

By Nancy Krulik

SCHOLASTIC INC.

New York   Toronto   London   Auckland   Sydney
Mexico City   New Delhi   Hong Kong   Buenos Aires

For Ian and Amanda, who have always lived for camp!

No part of this publication may be reproduced, stored in a retrieval system, or transmitted in any form or by any means, electronic, mechanical, photocopying, recording, or otherwise, without written permission of the publisher. For information regarding permission, write to Scholastic Inc., Attention: Permissions Department, 557 Broadway, New York, NY 10012.

ISBN-13: 978-0-545-09275-3
ISBN-10: 0-545-09275-2

Copyright © 2009 by Nancy Krulik.

Published by Scholastic Inc. All rights reserved.
SCHOLASTIC, APPLE PAPERBACKS, and associated logos are trademarks and/or registered trademarks of Scholastic Inc.

12 11 10 9 8 7 6 5 4 3 2   9 10 11 12 13 14/0

Printed in the U.S.A.
First printing, June 2009

Hey There, Old Sport!

Which is your idea of the perfect Saturday afternoon — catching a ball or catching forty winks? Are you a fitness fanatic or is your exercise of choice changing channels with the remote? This quick quiz will help you find out just how physical you really are.

1. *Brrrring!* The alarm goes off. Time to get up for school! How do you feel?

A. Like I want to roll over and take a nap.

B. A little groggy, but it's nothing a shower won't cure.

C. Ready for a brisk walk to school.

2. How often do you switch on the TV?

A. Only when there's something really good on.

B. Not very often. I'm too busy with my after-school activities.

C. It's always on in my room.

3. What's your take on gym class?

A. It's my favorite class of the day — I finally get to move!

B. Oh, man, I dread it!

C. Sometimes it's fun, but sometimes it's a real chore.

4. Saturday has finally arrived! Don't you just love the weekend? It's the perfect time to:

A. Hit the couch for cartoons and potato chips!

B. Get up and go for a run.

C. Go shopping.

5. When was the last time you had a workout that really made you sweat?

A. Last night.

B. Last week.

C. I do *not* sweat!

6. When you shop for workout clothes, what do you look for?

A. I don't buy workout clothes.

B. Something comfortable that I can move in.

C. Outfits that look cute out on the field.

7. What's your exercise schedule like?

A. I exercise a few times a week.

B. I have to get some exercise every day or I go crazy!

C. I only run if someone's chasing me.

8. What's hanging in your shoe organizer?

A. Heels! I love standing tall above the crowd.

B. Ballet flats, heels, and two pairs of running shoes.

C. Running shoes, hiking boots, swim fins, and cleats.

It's time to add up your score.

	A	B	C
1.	A) 1	B) 2	C) 3
2.	A) 2	B) 3	C) 1
3.	A) 3	B) 1	C) 2
4.	A) 1	B) 3	C) 2
5.	A) 3	B) 2	C) 1
6.	A) 1	B) 3	C) 2
7.	A) 2	B) 3	C) 1
8.	A) 1	B) 2	C) 3

So, what does your score say about you?

19-24 points: This is the score of champions! You are a major jock. Just be careful. You don't want to injure yourself by overdoing it.

13-18 points: You're a well-rounded girl! Keeping in shape is definitely important to you, but you manage to enjoy other activities besides sports, too.

8-12 points: Okay, Miss Couch Potato! It's time to discover that there are other things to crunch besides chips. Get up and get moving!

Chapter
ONE

- Five T-shirts
- Two long-sleeve shirts
- Two sweatshirts or sweaters
- One rain poncho
- Three pairs of jeans or running pants
- Two pairs of pajamas
- One hat
- Five pairs of socks
- Five pairs of underwear

I looked at the packing list that my science teacher had sent home with me the day before. The list seemed to be a mile long. I couldn't imagine how I was going to get all that stuff into my little suitcase. But I was going to have to figure it out. After all, I was going to be spending five days at Camp Einstein. I didn't want to get stuck there without enough underwear, socks, and bug spray. Especially the bug spray! There's nothing like a couple of huge mosquito bites to ruin a school trip.

That's what the visit to Camp Einstein was going to be. A *five-day* school field trip! All of the sixth and seventh graders at Joyce Kilmer Middle School were going to science camp together. (The eighth graders were going on a trip to Washington, D.C., later in the year.) I was really excited about the idea of spending a week at camp. So were all my friends. In fact, the science trip was pretty much all any of us had been talking about for the past week.

The seventh graders had already been on their first science camp trip last year, and they couldn't wait to tell the rest of us just how much fun it was. My friend Marc, who is a seventh grader, explained that science camp is just like regular camp, except you have to take notes and keep a journal. There are cabins to sleep in, a huge mess hall to eat in, and fun activities like hiking, pioneering, and toasting marshmallows over a campfire.

Some of my sixth grade friends were a little weirded out by the idea of spending a whole week away from home because they'd never done that before. They also weren't too crazy about the idea of sleeping in cabins in the woods, where there might be some wild animals lurking around. But I wasn't worried about anything. I'd already spent a whole summer at sleepaway camp. Five days was nothing to me. And as for sleeping on a cot in a cabin, I'd already done that, too. At Camp Kendale, I'd even slept in the woods in just a sleeping bag — no cabin, no cot, no tent. Just me, my sleeping bag, and the dirt. Actually it had been kind of comfortable and fun.

Especially in the morning when we'd made French toast over a campfire. That was the best breakfast I'd had all summer.

With all my camping experience, the only thing I found worrisome about the trip was this whole packing thing. At Camp Kendale, we'd worn uniforms — green-and-white camp T-shirts and shorts. But for our school camping trip, we were allowed to pack whatever we wanted to wear. That actually made things more difficult. I had to pick out clothes that were old enough that I didn't care if they got ruined or lost at camp, but cool enough to keep me from being teased by the Pops — our school's group of fashion police.

I think every school has its own group of Pops. That's Pop, as in *pop*ular. They're the girls who always have the coolest clothes, the newest cell phones, and the best makeup. They're the girls everyone would want to be if she could. But most girls can't, of course, because the Pops are a very exclusive group.

I learned that the hard way, when my former BFF, Addie Wilson, became a Pop. Somehow she managed to work her way into the exclusive group while I was away at camp last summer. By the time I got back, Addie was one of the queen bees at Joyce Kilmer Middle School. And unfortunately, there wasn't room for *me* in her hive.

Of course, losing Addie as a BFF didn't leave me friendless. I have a lot of friends — new friends. *Middle school friends.* We don't have the same history that Addie and I have (after all, Addie and I had been friends since kindergarten), but my new friends don't judge me or my clothes, my MP3 player, or my cell phone. They like me just because I'm me. And that's pretty cool. I was definitely glad my new friends were going to be on this camping trip with me. We were going to have a blast!

Speaking of blasts, my cell phone suddenly began blasting its ring loudly. The sound knocked thoughts about Addie out of my head and shot me back into reality. I glanced at the caller ID. It was my friend Sam.

"Hi, Sam," I greeted her.

"Hi, yourself, Jenny," Sam replied. "What are you up to?"

"Packing. Or rather *not* packing," I admitted. "I haven't put one thing in my suitcase."

"Me, neither," Sam said. "My mum and I just spent the past half hour arguing about whether or not I should bring sweatshirts or jumpers to camp."

I sighed. Sam and her mother were always arguing about something. It didn't mean they didn't love each other. That was just the kind of relationship they had. But I was a little confused about this argument.

"Why would you bring a jumper to camp?" I asked her. "The last thing you need at camp is a dress."

"No, not a jumper *dress*," Sam explained in her sophisticated British accent. "A wool jumper. You know, a sweater."

"Oh," I replied. "Another lost-in-translation problem."

Sam giggled. "Sometimes it's hard to believe we both speak the same language."

I laughed, too. "I know what you mean," I told her. "I didn't know there were two kinds of English until you moved here."

"Neither did I," Sam agreed. "You Yanks have certainly changed the language."

"I guess so," I told her. "Anyway, I think you should probably bring one of each. That's an easy compromise."

"You're right," Sam admitted. "A jumper and a sweat-shirt it is. Did you and your mum get a chance to go to the drugstore to pick up all your toiletries yet?"

"Oh, yeah. We got everything," I told Sam. "The shampoo I bought for the trip smells amazing. You can borrow it if you like."

"If we're in the same cabin," Sam pointed out.

"I think we will be," I said. "There are five people in a cabin. I put you, Chloe, Felicia, and Rachel on my bunking request list. That's five."

"I wrote down the same group of names," Sam told me. "Hopefully the teachers will put us with the people we requested."

"I think they will," I assured her.

"It's too bad we can't be with Liza and the twins, though," Sam pointed out. "I don't know why they won't let sixth and seventh graders be in the same cabins."

"I know. It's a definite bummer," I agreed. "But we'll

see them all day long." I paused for a second and glanced back at my empty suitcase. "I'll bet the seventh graders aren't having nearly the same trouble I am deciding what to bring. I mean they've done this already. They know what works and what doesn't."

"Well, you can't be having a harder time packing than the Pops must be having," Sam said. "It's not like they're going to be able to find a designer rain poncho at the mall."

"I'll bet they're freaking out about not being allowed to bring their hair dryers, flatirons, or cell phones," I added. "What's Addie going to do if she's not able to straighten her bangs every morning? And I don't know how Claire and Maya are going to be able to survive without cell phones to text each other constantly."

"You should talk," Sam teased. She giggled.

But I didn't get the joke. "What's that supposed to mean?" I asked her. "I hardly ever use my cell phone at school."

"No, you don't," Sam agreed. "But I don't know how you're going to survive five days without being able to go on the Internet."

"Oh, come on," I disagreed. "I spent all last summer without a computer."

"But that was before you discovered middleschool survival.com," Sam reminded me.

That was true. I hadn't found my favorite website until after I'd started sixth grade. And now I was hooked on it. I used the website for everything — recipes, fashion tips, jokes, and quizzes that told me things about my personality I'd never noticed before.

"I can go without middleschoolsurvival.com for five days," I insisted. But I didn't feel nearly as confident about that as I sounded. Now that Sam had brought it up, I wondered how I was going to survive a week of middle school science camp without my favorite site.

But before I could determine whether or not Sam believed what I'd said, I heard her mother calling her to come downstairs and pack up her things.

"Well, I've gotta run," she told me. "My mum is calling me."

"I should be packing, anyway," I told her. "I'll see you on the bus tomorrow."

"Bright and early," Sam agreed. "You want to sit with me?"

I could hear the usual confidence fade from Sam's voice. I had the feeling she was getting nervous about being away from home for five days. Not that I blamed her. Her family had moved here from England only a short while ago. It had taken her some time to get used to her new house, new school, and new friends. I could see why any change in her routine would be a little stressful for her, even if it was just for five days.

"I'll definitely sit with you on the bus," I assured her.

"Cool," she said happily. "Cheers, then."

As Sam hung up the phone, I sat back on my bed and thought about the conversation we'd just had. Was I really addicted to my computer? I didn't think I was. I mean, I did plenty of things that didn't involve a keyboard. I went to the mall and to the movies. I liked to ski. I was president of the sixth grade. And none of those things were done online.

Still, Sam wasn't completely wrong. I did spend an awful lot of time on the Internet. But that didn't mean that I was totally hooked on my computer. Did it?

Ironically, I could think of only one way to figure it out. And that was to go online and head straight for middleschoolsurvival.com. I figured there had to be a quiz on my favorite website that would help me determine just how attached to my computer I really was.

Sure enough, I was right. And with two clicks of my mouse, I was on my way to finding out the truth.

Are You Computer Crazed?

Is your motto *The one with the most bytes wins*? Are you one of those girls who checks her e-mail over and over again all day long? Do you find yourself clicking an imaginary mouse in your sleep? In other words, are you totally attached to your computer? There's only one way to find out. You've got to take the quiz. And lucky for you, it's right here on the computer!

1. **Your grandma is staying at your house for a few days, and she's fascinated by how adept you are at working on the computer. She tells you that when she was a kid, she wrote all of her homework by hand. How do you respond?**

A. You laugh and say, "No, seriously, Grandma, how did you do homework?"

B. You say, "Whoa, that must have been difficult."

Okay, that one was easy. I knew that computers hadn't been around forever. And I knew kids still had homework back then. It couldn't have been easy, though. At least not as easy as it was for me. I clicked the letter B, and the next question popped up on the screen.

2. What a rotten day! You bombed your French test, had a fight with your mom, and found out that the guy you like has a new girlfriend – who isn't you! It's time to chill out with some pals. Where do you go?

A. Straight to the computer. That way you can get sympathy and cheering up from a lot of people all at once.

B. To your BFF's house. This is a good day for some one-on-one face time with someone who really gets you.

That question was tougher than the first. I do like hanging out with my friends in person. But being cheered up online by a lot of friends is also very helpful when I'm down. My friends could send me jokes, funny pictures, and other things to cheer me up. And if I got tired of conversing, I could just type in a quick "G2G." Finally, I clicked the letter A and waited for the next question to appear.

3. Uh-oh! The second you arrive at your BFF's front door to pick her up for school, you realize you've left your cell phone at home. What do you do?

A. Run home and get it. You're only four blocks away.

B. Ring the doorbell and make a mental note to check your texts and voice mails when you get home.

I have to have my cell phone. And not just because it keeps me in touch with all my friends. What if my mom or dad needed to tell me something? Or what if someone in my class was absent from school that day and had to know what the homework was right away? Okay, no one in sixth grade is that anxious to do homework, but I'd probably run home and get my phone if I could. So I clicked the letter A and moved on.

4. You just had the most incredible birthday party. The gifts you got were totally awesome. How do you thank everyone?

A. With a mass e-mail — you want your friends to know how grateful you are for their thoughtfulness ASAP!

B. You send out individual handwritten notes. It might take longer, but it's more personal.

I wasn't exactly sure how to answer this question. Chances are I would want to send e-mails out to my friends to thank them. But I would never send a mass e-mail. I'd send them each a personal one. Still, I probably wouldn't send handwritten notes. I don't know anyone who does that anymore. In the end, I decided that my answer was closer to A than it was to B. So I clicked the letter A (with reservations) and waited for the next question to appear.

5. When it comes to the Internet, you:

A. Use it to talk to your friends, send jokes to people, and watch videos.

B. Use it for research only.

This one was easier for me to answer than the question before it. Sure, I did research on the Internet. But I didn't use it for that exclusively. I definitely spent more time chatting with friends and downloading funny videos. Not only that, but my friends and I had done some webcasts over the Internet. So as far as I was concerned, the Internet was a lot more than just a research tool. I clicked the letter A.

The computer took a moment to compute my score. Then, finally, it appeared.

You have answered: 4 As and 1 B.
So what do your answers say about you?

4-5 As: You are a total techie! You love anything that's hooked to a modem or working with wireless. Face it. You're addicted!

2-3 As: Congratulations! You've found the perfect middle ground. You like technology, and you recognize that it helps you in your day-to-day life, but you can survive without it — at least for a while.

0-1 As: Hello? Have you heard that this is the twenty-first century? Computers can be your friends — as long as you use them in moderation and still keep up face-to-face contact with creatures that don't have keyboards attached!

I gulped. According to the quiz, I was definitely obsessed with my computer. And that obviously wasn't a good thing. For a minute, I thought about searching middleschoolsurvival.com for another quiz on the same subject. Maybe if I took that quiz, I'd get a different result.

But searching the website would just be proving the quiz's point. There was only one thing for me to do. I clicked off the computer and went back to my packing list. After all, packing my suitcase was something middleschoolsurvival.com would not be able to help me with.

Chapter
TWO

AS IT TURNED OUT, I wasn't going to have to be completely separated from my favorite website for a whole week after all. I learned that the next morning, as my friends and I waited outside the school for the bus to Camp Einstein.

"I did a lot of research on Camp Einstein last week," my friend Josh told us. "This is going to be the most incredible week. You wouldn't believe all the stuff they have there. They have a huge telescope for astronomy, an animal-filled nature shack, a chemistry lab, geology study hikes, leaf and flower identification hikes, a state-of-the-art computer center . . ."

Sam prodded me in the side. "Bet that makes you happy," she teased.

"I'm not spending all of my time on the computer," I assured her. "I want to go on some hikes. I love being out in the woods. I can't wait to get to camp!"

There were some people waiting for the bus who didn't share my enthusiasm, though. The Pops were all standing in a cluster, and they looked miserable. Sabrina was even crying.

"What's with her?" Chloe asked.

"She's an eighth grader," Marilyn answered.

"So she's not going on this trip," her sister Carolyn explained.

"She'll be all alone at the Pop table during fifth period lunch," the twins said together.

"And you know she won't lower herself to eat at anyone else's table," Josh added.

"Correction. No one else would lower themselves to let *her* eat at *their* table," Chloe said smugly.

My friends giggled. But I didn't. I actually felt bad for Sabrina. I'd had to eat lunch alone a few times. It was at the beginning of the school year, when I didn't have any of my new friends. I just sort of wandered the cafeteria, looking for a familiar face. It got so bad that I actually spent the whole lunch period in the phone booth one day so no one would realize I didn't have anyone to eat with.

Then suddenly I remembered something else about that day. The reason I'd had to eat alone was because Addie and her new Pop friends — including Sabrina — had refused to let me eat at their table. Suddenly I didn't feel so bad for her anymore. In fact, I thought it might be a good thing for her to eat alone for a few days. Maybe she would learn one of the main rules I'd discovered after weeks of being in middle school. It wasn't a rule in the official middle school handbook. It was one that I'd added to my ever-growing list of rules you have to learn all on your own.

MIDDLE SCHOOL RULE #33:

TRY TO BE FRIENDLY TO EVERYONE. YOU NEVER KNOW WHEN SOMEONE YOU'VE BEEN KIND TO WILL BE THE ONE YOU NEED TO HELP YOU THROUGH A TOUGH TIME.

I knew for a fact that #33 was a rule Sabrina hadn't followed. And because of that, she would probably be eating her lunch in a phone booth, or in the library, or even in the girls' bathroom for the next five days. But I didn't have much time to think about Sabrina. At just that moment, the bus pulled into the parking lot. It was time to head to Camp Einstein.

"Okay, Jen-Jen, this is it," my mother said, using one of her many pet names for me. I flinched a little, wondering if any of my friends had heard. But if they had, they weren't saying. I relaxed a little, realizing that they were all being hugged and kissed by their parents, too. And there were plenty of pet names flying around the parking lot.

"This is it, m'love, time to go," Sam's mom was saying. "Are you sure you don't need a few quid just in case?"

"No, Mum, I don't need any money," Sam assured her. "There's nothing to buy up there."

"Okay, Felicia," I heard Mrs. Liguori tell my friend. "Don't do anything I wouldn't do."

"Joshie, I'm going to e-mail you," Josh's mom assured him. "Every day, just like I promised. They're going to print out the e-mails and distribute them at mail call."

I heard Josh sigh heavily, but he didn't say anything. In fact, we were all doing a lot of sighing. It was kind of embarrassing to have our moms hug and kiss us like this. But it seemed like everyone in the sixth and seventh grade had to endure it. And because of that, no one was all that embarrassed.

At least none of *my* friends were. Out of the corner of my eye, I could see the Pops were having a very different reaction to the good-bye scene. They wanted nothing to do with their moms and dads. They were practically shriveling at their touch, and I swear I saw Dana wipe one of her mother's kisses off of her cheek. Obviously, they thought it looked really babyish to have their parents hug and kiss them good-bye. The weird thing was, their reactions made them look even more babyish than the rest of us. The grownup thing to do would have been to just grin and bear it.

A few minutes later, and the hugs, kisses, and pet names were just a memory. We were loaded onto our buses and sent on our way. Good-bye, Joyce Kilmer Middle School; hello, Camp Einstein!

"We're supposed to have really clear weather tonight and tomorrow," Josh said, turning slightly so he was facing Felicia, who was sitting next to him, and Sam and me, who were sitting just behind him. "That's great, because we'll be able to see both the Big Dipper and the Little Dipper through the giant telescope they have up at camp."

"I didn't know you were into astronomy," Sam said.

"Josh is into all kinds of science," Felicia said proudly. "He reads science books just for fun."

I grinned. Felicia was so proud of her boyfriend. Just being around him made her happy.

But there were some people on the bus who were definitely less impressed with Josh's love of all things scientific. Addie and Dana were sitting two rows in front of Josh. They'd heard everything he'd said. "Thanks for the astronomy update, Mr. Science Geek," Dana remarked drolly.

Addie began to laugh. "Mr. Science Geek, that's a good one," she chuckled.

Dana smiled proudly and laughed even harder.

Personally, I thought Mr. Science Geek was actually a pretty stupid name to call someone, but judging from the way Addie and Dana were laughing, I had a feeling I'd be hearing the same joke all week long. Once the Pops found someone to pick on, they stuck with it. One week my friend Chloe had been their victim, and they'd spent days trying to convince people she had a secret romance she wasn't telling us about. And that was in between making all sorts of rude comments about her clothes and her hair.

As for me, well, I'd been their victim plenty of times, too. I guess that's because Addie hates me about as much now as she used to like me back when we were BFFs in elementary school. She will stop at nothing to embarrass me, and she's actually pretty good at it. Even though it was months ago, I still turn red when I think about the way the Pops wrote me anonymous secret admirer notes, just to see if I would fall for their trick and really think some boy at school liked me. I did fall for it, which is what made the whole thing even worse.

Compared to all of that, Josh was getting off pretty easy. Being called Mr. Science Geek for a week wasn't all that awful. Besides, Josh didn't seem to mind. He'd ignored Dana's comments and was now explaining constellations to us.

Once Addie and Dana realized their jokes weren't getting under Josh's skin, they stopped laughing and went back to ignoring him. They pulled their makeup bags from their backpacks and started putting on eye shadow.

"I don't know why they're putting on eye makeup," I whispered to Sam. "It's camp! No one wears makeup at camp!"

"Maybe they just want to fit in," Sam said.

"Fit in?" I asked. "With who?"

"With the raccoons," Sam told me. "Did you ever notice how all that mascara and eyeliner makes Dana look like a raccoon?"

That really made me laugh — especially because it was so true! I leaned back in my seat and stared out the window. Already the view had changed. We weren't passing any shopping malls or car dealerships on the road, like we had when we had been closer to home. Now all I could see for miles were trees, and a couple of billboards. Then something else caught my eye.

"Hey, guys!" I said excitedly. "That sign we just passed said CAMP EINSTEIN, NEXT EXIT. We're almost there!"

Chapter
THREE

I COULDN'T BELIEVE MY EARS. We'd only just arrived at Camp Einstein and already things were going terribly wrong. My science teacher, Mrs. Johnson, had just finished reading the cabin lists out loud. I was in a cabin with Sam and Chloe, which was great. But Rachel and Felicia weren't with us. Instead, Sam, Chloe, and I were going to be sharing a cabin with Addie Wilson and Dana Harrison.

"This is *not* good," I muttered to Sam and Chloe as we carried our luggage over to Cabin 7.

"Maybe they'll let us switch," Sam suggested hopefully.

Chloe shook her head. "Remember what Mrs. Johnson said." Chloe pursed her lips and lowered her voice an octave to imitate Mrs. Johnson's tone. "These rooming assignments are nonnegotiable."

Sam and I laughed. Once again, Chloe had done a spot-on imitation of one of our teachers.

"Besides, it's three of us and only two of them," Chloe reminded us. "They don't stand a chance."

In the regular world, Chloe would have been right — three beats two every time. But this wasn't the regular world. This was the *middle school* world. And in our world,

Pops were more powerful than non-Pops no matter what the numbers. It was just the way it was.

Still, I wasn't going to let the Pops ruin my week at camp. I'd been looking forward to this for too long to let that happen. "Come on, you guys," I said to Sam and Chloe. "Let's hurry to the cabin. We don't want to get the beds closest to the bathroom." (That was a little rule they don't tell you in the *camp* handbook.)

Chloe, Sam, and I beat Addie and Dana to the cabin by a long shot because, as I'd predicted, they'd *way* over-packed their suitcases. Since the teachers said we all had to carry our own luggage, those heavy bags put them at a definite disadvantage. By the time they arrived at the cabin, the only beds left were the bunk beds closest to the bathroom. Chloe and I were sharing the bunk bed near the windows, and Sam had taken the cot beside us.

"I've always wanted to sleep on a top bunk," Chloe told me with a hopeful look.

"Take it," I told her.

"Are you sure?" Chloe said. "Because if you also want the top, we can each have it for two nights, or we can do rock-paper-scissors, or . . ."

"It's fine, Chlo," I assured my friend. "I slept in a top bunk all last summer at camp. You take it for the week."

"Cool!" Chloe exclaimed. She raced up the ladder to her bed and bounced around a few times on the thin camp mattress. "These beds are going to be a little uncomfortable," she told us.

"You get used to it," I assured her.

"I guess," Chloe agreed. She turned and looked out the window. "Wow! I have such a great view from here."

Addie rolled her eyes. "It's not like you're at the top of the Empire State Building looking down on New York City, Chloe," she reminded her. "You have a view of the grass and the mess hall. Big deal."

"A view of the grass and the mess hall is better than a view of the loo," Sam told Addie. "Which, I believe, is all you can see from your bed."

Addie sighed. "I couldn't care less," she told Sam. Then she opened her suitcase and began placing her clothes into the cubby beside her. I have to admit I was watching her out of the corner of my eye. I was curious to see what kind of clothes a Pop would bring on a camping trip.

I wasn't surprised when the designer jeans came out of her suitcase. I'd brought mostly running pants and shorts, because that was what was most comfortable on hikes. But I figured Addie and Dana wouldn't be comfortable in anything as unstylish as running pants, no matter where they were.

What *did* surprise me was something *Dana* pulled out of her suitcase. I couldn't believe my eyes. "You aren't allowed to have hair straighteners here," I told Dana. "It said so right on the packing list."

"Don't be such a goody-goody," Dana snapped back. "Do you always follow the rules?"

Yeah, actually, I do. But I didn't tell her that. Instead I

said, "There's a reason they don't want electric appliances in the cabins. They use up too much electricity. If everyone brought their hair straighteners, the lights could go out all over the camp!"

"But everybody *didn't* bring their hair straighteners," Dana answered. "I'm the only one who did. So there's no problem."

Grrr. Dana really made me angry sometimes. I couldn't believe how incredibly self-centered she was.

"Oh, and I brought my blow-dryer, too," Dana added smugly. "I don't go anywhere without it."

"By the way," Addie said, looking pointedly at Sam, Chloe, and me. "If any of the teachers finds out about the hair straightener or the blow-dryer, we'll know you guys were the ones who told. And believe me, you don't want the whole grade knowing you squeal!"

Addie was right about that. Telling on someone was just about the worst thing you could do in middle school. Come to think of it, it was that way in elementary school, too. And I suspected being a tattletale in high school wouldn't make you too popular, either.

"Come on, Jenny, finish unpacking," Chloe said, obviously trying to distract me from the argument. "Sam and I are practically done. I want to get out there and explore this place."

I nodded. Chloe was right. Arguing with Addie and Dana was a lost cause. And there was a whole camp out there to explore. Quickly, I threw the last of my T-shirts in the cubby, pulled my hair back, and raced out of the cabin. I was happy to leave Addie, Dana, and their hair straightener to themselves.

"Camp food's made of ooey-gooey gopher guts, mutilated monkey meat, chopped-up canary feet . . ." Marc and I sang at the top of our lungs as we sat at the table in the Camp Einstein mess hall. Besides his week at Camp Einstein, Marc had been to summer sleepaway camp, too, so he knew all the same songs I did.

"Okay, that's just gross," Liza said, but she was giggling, anyway.

Luckily, the camp food was better than we'd expected. Our first lunch was pizza bagels and chicken soup, with orange slices for dessert. Not bad for a camp meal. It was actually better than what they served at the school cafeteria.

"The Pops look absolutely all at sixes and sevens," Sam said, pointing across the table to where Addie, Dana, Claire, and Maya were sitting.

"All what?" Liza asked her.

"At sixes and sevens," Sam repeated. "You know, kind of confused and out of their element."

"That's probably because they'd have to leave the mess hall to go to the girls' room," Marilyn pointed out. "Which means . . ."

"They can't gossip in their private meeting place," Carolyn added, finishing her sister's thought.

We all knew what the twins were talking about. The Pops always spent at least half of fifth period lunch hanging out in the girls' bathroom. They used it like a clubhouse. It was where they put on makeup, and then talked about everyone else in the school. I don't know if not having a place to gossip in private was what was bothering the Pops, but they certainly didn't seem as happy as my friends and I were to be at Camp Einstein.

I looked across the table at Rachel and burst out laughing. She'd managed to take a whole orange slice and shove it into her mouth, so it was sitting in front of her teeth. It was like she had a big, giant orange smile. She looked hilarious.

"Pretty," Chloe teased her. "You've never looked better."

Josh laughed and popped a slice into his mouth as well. A minute later, we were all sitting there with big orange-peel smiles. We looked so funny that a few kids at the next table started doing it as well.

"Hey, Rach, I never knew you were such a trendsetter," I said, taking the orange slice out of my mouth so I could talk.

Rachel took her slice out, too. "*Orange* you glad I'm at your lunch table today?"

I nodded happily. I really was glad Felicia and Rachel were eating lunch with us this week. They were the only two of my friends who didn't have fifth period lunch. I always felt like they were missing out by not being with the rest of us. "And we'll get to eat breakfast and dinner together, too," I reminded her.

"This is going to be the best week!" Felicia exclaimed happily.

Well, it certainly started out that way. Right after lunch, my friends and I all signed up to go on a nature hike that afternoon. We were going to walk through the woods, checking out all the plants and animals around the camp. The nature counselors were even going to give us each a pair of binoculars so we could check out the birds way up in the trees.

Chloe, Sam, and I went back to our cabin to put on hiking boots for the trek. Addie and Dana were already there when we arrived. They were putting on shorts and T-shirts for the activity they'd signed up for, nature at the lake.

"There are probably some really cool animals down by the lake," I said to them, in an attempt to be nice. I figured since we were going to be sharing a cabin for a whole week, we might as well try to get along.

Unfortunately, Addie and Dana were not in the same cease-fire mood I was. Dana rolled her eyes at me. "Oh, please," she said. "Like we're really going to sit there and stare at some turtles sunning themselves on a rock all afternoon. We're just going there because it's the best place to get a tan."

I knew they were never going to get away with that. We all had journals, and we were supposed to write down the things we learned at each activity. We were going to be graded on the journal. There was no way the Camp Einstein nature counselors or Mrs. Johnson were going to let Addie and Dana just lie on a dock all afternoon studying the effects of the rays of the sun on their skin.

"Uh, nice shoes, Jenny," Addie sneered as she looked down at my camel-colored hiking boots. "A little clunky, don't you think?"

"They're supposed to be," I told her. "They're sturdy. And comfortable. That's what you need to wear when you go hiking in the woods."

"Ick, the woods!" Dana exclaimed. "There are so many disgusting animals out there, like snakes, slugs, and field mice."

"Oh, Jenny won't mind the field mice," Addie told Dana. "She already lives with two mice right in her room."

"Ooo! Gross me out," Dana said. "I hate mice!"

That was okay by me. I had a feeling my pet mice wouldn't like Dana Harrison too much, either. Animals usually have a good sense of whether someone is a kind person.

I could tell from the look on Sam's face, though, that it was not okay with her. She'd clearly had enough of Addie and Dana. "I'd rather share a space with two mice than you two ugly street rats!" she exclaimed angrily.

"Who are you calling a rat?" Addie demanded.

Chloe giggled. "She's right, Sam," she said.

Sam and I stared at her. Was Chloe actually defending Addie Wilson?

"I mean, why would you insult a rat by comparing it to *her*?" Chloe added. I smiled. That was more like the Chloe I knew and loved.

"Don't you dare call me a rat," Addie said in a threatening tone.

But Sam wasn't about to back off. "Hey, if the beady eyes fit . . ." Sam stared directly at Addie as she let her voice drift off.

"My eyes are not beady!" Addie shouted back. "And you . . ."

But before Addie could finish her sentence, we heard a loud whistle blow. It was time to head out to our first activities. And boy, was I glad. It was nice of my friends to defend me, but I really wanted all the arguing to stop. Sure, Sam and Chloe may have put Addie in her place for now, but I knew Addie better than they did. She never let anyone get the last word. If we made her angry, she'd be sure to make us miserable. And the last thing I wanted to be at science camp was miserable.

Chapter
FOUR

"I AM SO TIRED," Sam moaned as she plopped down on her cot after our hike.

"Me, too," I agreed. "But I'm glad we went on that hike."

"I've never been that high up before — at least not without being in an airplane," Chloe added. "I swear you could see for miles up there. What a view from the top of that mountain!"

"What is it with you and views?" Dana said as she toweled off her hair and walked out of the bathroom. "Do you have a thing about being up in space or something?"

"More like she's a space *cadet*," Addie said with a giggle. Dana started laughing.

Chloe rolled her eyes, and then went on, basically ignoring everything Dana and Addie were saying. "I loved when we stopped and got a chance to write in our journals at the top of the mountain," she continued. "I was so inspired! I wrote four poems."

"I wrote a descriptive paragraph," I said. "I used as many adjectives as I could to describe the majestic, fantastic, overwhelming vision of the rocky mountains and tall, swaying trees."

"That sounds totally brill," Sam complimented me. "I just sketched a few things around me – plants, flowers, and a couple of pine trees clumped together. I thought my drawings were pretty good – until I saw Liza's. She drew this butterfly sitting on a flower that was the most gorgeous thing I'd ever seen."

"When it comes to art, Liza's in a class by herself," I told Sam. "I'm sure your drawings were good, too."

Sam shrugged. "I did like the one I did of those baby birds in the tree."

"How cute were they?" I asked her. "And didn't you just love when the mother bird brought them a worm to eat? It was amazing to watch her chew it up and then spit the pieces into their mouths."

"Ooo, chewed-up worms. That's totally gross," Dana said. "I can't listen to any more of this." She turned to Sam, Chloe, and me. "I'm sure you won't mind if I drown you out," she added. Then she plugged her hair dryer into one of the two sockets in the cabin wall and began to dry her hair. A moment later, Addie plugged the hair straightener into the other socket and began to straighten her bangs.

"Do you believe those two?" Sam asked Chloe and me. "You'd think this was some sort of beauty contest instead of science camp."

"Forget about them," Chloe told her. "We've got more important things to think about. Remember, tomorrow we've got arts and crafts."

I smiled. Art project day was definitely going to be fun. We each had to come up with an art project to do on our own. But you couldn't just make a box with Popsicle sticks or string some beads together like you would at regular camp. Here at science camp, you had to come up with a project you could do using materials that could be found in nature.

"Liza, Josh, and Felicia are going to use plants and flowers to make naturally colored paints," Sam said. "And I think Marc is taking pictures with his digital camera to create a collage of pictures of plant life."

"He is," Chloe replied. "And the twins and Rachel were thinking of making one of those Native American dream catcher things with feathers they found on the ground during the hike."

"So that just leaves the three of us with no ideas for projects," I pointed out.

"I can't come up with anything," Chloe said.

"Me, neither," Sam agreed. "But I guess we could join in and do something our friends are doing. The dream catchers would be pretty."

"Or we could go to the computer science center after dinner and see if middleschoolsurvival.com has any ideas for a nature art project," I suggested.

"I knew you couldn't stay away from that website for very long," Sam teased me. Then she added, "But that's actually a great idea."

"Thanks," I replied. "So right after dinner we'll —" But I didn't get to finish my sentence. Because at just that moment, Dana's blow-dryer went silent, the orange light on the hair straightener turned off, and the overhead light in the cabin went out.

"What happened?" Dana asked angrily.

"I think you blew a fuse," I told her. "These old cabins don't have great wiring. I told you there was a reason they didn't want us bringing blow-dryers and hair straighteners to camp."

"Well, what are we supposed to do now?" Dana demanded. "I can't go to dinner this way. Only half my head is dry."

"I guess we'll have to tell someone on Camp Einstein's staff. They'll fix it," I told her.

"You can't do that," Addie objected. "Then they'll know Dana brought this stuff to camp. She'll get in trouble."

"You mean *we'll* get in trouble," Dana reminded her. "We were both using them."

"But they're both yours," Addie reminded her.

"Well, we have to do something," Sam told Addie and Dana. "Otherwise we won't have a light in here all week."

"So what?" Addie asked. "We have flashlights for nighttime, and during the day we can just use sunlight." She handed the hair straightener to Dana. "It's cooled off. I was only able to straighten my bangs."

Dana shoved the straightener and the blow-dryer in her suitcase and shut it tight. Obviously, she was hiding the evidence.

"That's ridiculous," Chloe insisted. "I don't care if you guys get in trouble. I'm going to get someone to help us."

"You'd better not," Dana said. She glared at Chloe.

The look in Dana's eyes scared me. But not Chloe. She wasn't the least bit frightened of Dana. In fact, she laughed right in her face. "Give me a break," she scoffed as she headed toward the door of the cabin.

But before Chloe could even get out the door, Mrs. Johnson appeared at our cabin. "Girls, someone has blown a fuse," she said. "This cabin and those on either side of it are without power. Has anyone in here been using electrical items?"

Dana and Addie glared in Chloe's direction. Chloe glared back. But she didn't say anything. Instead, Dana spoke.

"No, Mrs. Johnson," she said in a sweet voice. "It wasn't us."

Mrs. Johnson nodded slowly. She looked at each of us, and then nodded slowly. "Really?" she asked. She smiled at Dana. "Interesting hairdo," she said.

Dana's face paled. Apparently she'd forgotten that only one side of her head was dry. The other was sopping wet.

"How did you manage to get only one side of your head dry?" Mrs. Johnson asked Dana pointedly.

Dana looked down and kicked at the floor. She didn't say a word. What could she say? She'd been caught and she knew it.

"Hand over the dryer, Dana," Mrs. Johnson said firmly. "And any other electrical items you might have, as well. I'll give them back to *your parents* when they pick you up at the bus on Friday afternoon."

Now Dana looked nervous. We all knew that was Mrs. Johnson's way of letting her know that she was going to tell Dana's parents about her breaking the rules. Dana definitely didn't want to get in any more trouble. So she opened her suitcase and handed the hair dryer and the straightener to our science teacher.

"Addie, your hair looks awfully nice," Mrs. Johnson said. "Your bangs are so straight, while the rest of your hair is curly. I guess you've been playing beauty parlor today as well. It's amazing how well those hair straighteners work, isn't it?"

Addie shrugged quietly and then, like Dana, stared at the floor.

Mrs. Johnson looked at Chloe, Sam, and me. I guess it was pretty obvious that we had all just come in from our hike, because we were still sweaty and messy. Chloe even had a few stray leaves in her hair. Our science teacher knew right away that we hadn't been using hair dryers or hair straighteners. So she turned her attention back to Addie and Dana.

"You two girls need to learn to follow the rules," Mrs. Johnson told them. "So tonight, you're going to help the kitchen staff clean up after everyone eats dinner. I'm sure they have plenty of rules about how the mess hall has to be mopped up."

"Mopped?" Addie's voice scaled up nervously as she spoke. "But, Mrs. Johnson, tonight we have free time and my friends and I were planning on —"

"Forget free time, Addie," Mrs. Johnson said. "You gave that up the minute you straightened your bangs. Now I have to go and find someone to fix the fuse you girls blew. I'll see all of you at dinner in half an hour."

As the door swung shut behind Mrs. Johnson, Addie and Dana glared at Chloe, Sam, and me. I had a feeling they were trying to think of a way to blame this on us. But they couldn't, and they knew it.

"What am I going to do about my hair?" Dana moaned.

"Just wet your whole head again in the sink," Addie told her. "Then I'll French braid it."

"French braiding is an awful lot of work, Addie," Chloe said. "But I guess it's worth it. Dana will want to look her best while she's scrubbing down the tables and throwing bags of garbage into the smelly Dumpsters."

Sam and I burst out laughing. Addie and Dana did not laugh one bit. Obviously, they just didn't appreciate Chloe's sense of humor the way we did.

*   *   *

After dinner, Chloe, Sam, and I went over to the computer center to try to find an interesting art project we could do with natural objects that could be found at Camp Einstein. The room was pretty full, but we managed to find an open computer toward the back of the wooden cabin.

I sat down and typed in middleschoolsurvival.com. It took a few seconds, but eventually our favorite website appeared on the computer screen.

"How about leaf printing?" I asked, scrolling down the list of nature crafts the website offered.

"I did that in third grade," Chloe complained.

"It's not as cool as some of the other projects kids are doing," Sam agreed. "What else do they have on the website?"

"Painted rock paperweights?" I suggested.

Sam shook her head. "Who wants to lug a bunch of painted rocks home? My suitcase is heavy enough."

"Wait a minute. I think I've found the perfect craft!" I exclaimed happily. I moved to the side to give Chloe and Sam a better view of what I was looking at.

"Sand candles! Sweet!" Sam cheered. "This is the perfect project."

"Totally," Chloe agreed. "Everyone is going to want to make one."

"It shouldn't be hard to get all the things we'll need," I said as I scanned the list of materials. "I know there's wax in the arts and crafts shack. I saw it when we passed by on the way to the woods for our hike."

"And there's plenty of sand down by the lake," Sam added.

"We're all set," Chloe said excitedly.

Once again my favorite website had come through. Except for one thing. "It says we need an adult for this," I told my friends. "I guess that's because of the hot wax."

"That's okay. There are about a zillion adults around here. Between the teachers and the counselors, someone will help us," Chloe assured me.

"Okay, then," I said. "All I have to do is print out the directions, and we're all set."

Super Sand Candles!

You can use sand to make something really special that lasts a lot longer than a sand castle! A sand candle.

YOU WILL NEED:

One gallon of sand, water, wax (the amount of wax you'll need will depend on the size of the candle you want to make), shells, string (this needs to be long enough to reach the bottom of the sand candle, with room for a wick at the top), an empty tin can, a bowl, and an adult who will help you with the hot wax.

HERE'S WHAT YOU DO:

1. Put the sand in a large bowl and pour water over the sand. Make sure it is very wet, but not flooded. The less water you use, the thicker the outside of your sand candle will be.

2. Make a hole in the wet sand that is as big as you want your candle to be.

3. Place shells around the sides of the hole if desired.

4. Tie the smallest shell to the string. (This will be your wick.) Place it in the center at the bottom of the hole.

5. Ask an adult to melt the wax in a tin can.

6. Ask an adult to pour the hot wax into the sand mold while holding the wick up to keep it straight.

7. Ask an adult to hold the wick there until the wax has hardened enough for the wick to not fall into the candle. This should only take a minute or two.

8. When your wax candle is hard and cold (this will take a few hours), gently dig a trench in the sand. Be sure to stay about an inch away from the candle all around. Then *gently* pull the candle out and brush off any loose sand.

Once we had the directions printed out, Sam, Chloe, and I left the computer center. It was only fair. There was a long line of kids who wanted to use the computers that night — apparently I wasn't the only one who missed the feeling of the keyboard under her fingers. I figured that place would be busy all the way up until it was time for lights-out.

"I wonder where everyone else went," Chloe said as we walked back outside.

We didn't have to wait long to find Marc. He literally popped up in front of us, with his video camera in hand. Marc is never far from his video camera. He wants to be a film director one day, and right now he's busy making a documentary about middle school life. The way he describes it, it's like MTV's *The Real World*, but it takes place in middle school.

"I'm shooting some footage for the film club," he explained. "We're going to show it at the orientation assembly for next year's incoming sixth graders."

"Cool!" Chloe exclaimed. She leaped in front of the camera, eager for a chance to perform. "My name is Chloe. And I'm going to take you on a tour of Camp Einstein by night."

Marc laughed, but he didn't shut off the camera. Apparently Chloe's never-ending desire to perform in front of a camera worked for him.

Sam and I walked behind Marc as he filmed Chloe-the-tour-guide. We stopped when we reached the astronomy center. It didn't surprise me that we found Josh and Felicia there. Josh had been talking about using the giant tele-scope all day long. Now that it was dark out, he was the first one in line. Actually, he and Felicia were the *only* ones in line. Most of the other kids were busy singing camp songs at the giant bonfire or waiting in line at the computer center. But those weren't the kinds of things that interested Josh. He was really into the *science* part of science camp. And somehow, he'd managed to get Felicia interested in that, too.

"Do you see that reddish star?" he asked Felicia as she put her eye up against the telescope. "That's not really a star. It's Mars."

"Why does it look red?" Felicia asked him.

"The soil is made of iron oxide, which has a reddish color," Josh explained.

"Blimey, is there anything you don't know?" Sam asked him with a laugh.

Even in the dark, I could see Josh blushing — in fact, he turned the color of Mars. I could sympathize with him. I'm a champion blusher, too. Whenever anyone gives me a compliment, or makes me stand out in any way, I can feel that old familiar feeling running up into my cheeks.

Just then, I spotted Addie and Dana walking toward us on their way to the cabin. At least I thought it was Addie and Dana. It was hard to tell. They certainly didn't look like any Pops I'd ever seen. Dana's French braid was a mess — half her hair had fallen out of the braid and was dangling in front of her face. Addie was all sweaty, and her eye makeup was running down her cheeks, kind of like bright blue zebra stripes.

I figured they were hurrying to the cabin to change before anyone could see them. Not that I blamed them. If it were me, I'd be hiding behind trees to keep from being spotted looking like that.

But Addie and Dana weren't like me at all. And apparently, they weren't hiding from anyone. In fact, as soon as they spotted us standing around the telescope, they stopped and began to laugh.

"Check it out. Mr. Science Geek is giving a lecture," Dana giggled.

"Do you like the *view* from the telescope, Chloe?" Addie teased. "It's perfect for a space cadet like you."

I rolled my eyes. Addie and Dana kept using the same lame jokes over and over. "You guys are getting kind of boring," I told them in an attempt to stand up for my friends.

Addie sighed. "No. Boring is hanging around Mr. Science Geek," she told me.

"And don't forget *Mrs.* Science Geek," Dana added, pointing to Felicia.

I didn't have to look at Josh to know that Dana's comment had made him blush all over again. Josh knew that everyone knew he and Felicia were boyfriend and girlfriend. He just didn't like when anybody talked about it.

But Felicia didn't care who knew, or who said anything about it. She especially didn't care what Pops like Addie and Dana thought. "At least we don't smell like a Dumpster," she told them. "What happened? Did the kitchen staff try to throw you in with the rest of the garbage?"

That stopped Addie and Dana in their tracks. They were genuinely shocked that anyone had dared to speak to them that way. But they got their bearings back pretty quickly.

"We're going to take showers now, Felicia," Dana informed her. "And then we'll be clean and beautiful again. But no shower in the world can wash away geekiness! You'll be stuck with it forever."

And with that, she and Addie walked off, giggling as they went.

"I can't believe you guys were ever friends with Addie Wilson," Chloe said to Felicia and me.

I knew what she meant. Felicia, Rachel, Addie, and I had all gone to the same elementary school. We'd all been friends there. But of course, there were no Pops in elementary school. And back then, Addie had been really nice. Not that I could tell Chloe that. She wouldn't believe me. If I were her, I wouldn't have believed it, either. Not with the way Addie acted now.

Still, it was pretty impressive the way Addie and Dana had been able to stand there and talk to us, despite the fact that they looked and smelled awful. Apparently you could be a Pop even when you didn't look like one.

Which made me realize something. For the first time, the Pops had introduced me to a middle school rule that wasn't written in the official school handbook. And as upsetting as it was for me to have learned something from Addie and Dana, I silently added the new rule to my list, anyway.

MIDDLE SCHOOL RULE #34:
CONFIDENCE DOESN'T COME FROM WHAT YOU'RE WEARING OR HOW YOU LOOK. IT COMES FROM HOW YOU FEEL ABOUT YOURSELF ON THE INSIDE.

That was one rule Addie and Dana knew well – *too* well, in fact. As usual, they had crossed the line from confident to obnoxious.

But now that they'd moved on, my friends and I could forget about them. There were much more interesting things to focus on – like the stars, and the smell of smoke and toasted marshmallows wafting up from the bonfire by the lake. I could hear Mr. Sabatino – the sixth grade music teacher – playing his guitar while kids sang along.

"I think they're making s'mores!" Sam squealed. "Those are my favorite." She turned to Josh and Felicia. "Sorry, you guys, but I need a sweet. And I need it now." And with that, Sam raced off toward the campfire.

Chloe and I weren't far behind. Sam wasn't the only one who was in the mood to cook a few marshmallows over an open fire. The ooey-gooey goodness was calling to me, too.

Chapter
FIVE

"I CAN'T WAIT TO SEE our sand candles when they're finished!" Chloe exclaimed as she, Sam, and I walked back into the cabin after our nature craft period the next morning. We had to wash off the sand before lunch. I figured that was going to take a while, since we'd been down at the beach most of the morning, putting sand in buckets, arranging shells, and pouring in wax. I'm not sure how I got sand in my hair, shirt, and underwear, but I'd managed. And I was eager to get in the shower.

"I wonder if the shells are really going to stick," Sam called to me through the bathroom door. "I think I might have put too many of them in the sand."

"The wax should hold them in place," I called back to her. "Besides, your candle will be pretty no matter what. I love the purple wax you used."

"Hey, hurry up in there," Chloe shouted. "There's only one shower, and three of us. I'm pretty sandy out here."

"I'm coming," I said, stepping out of the shower and wrapping my terry cloth robe around me. "It's all yours, Chlo."

Just then, Addie and Dana wandered into the cabin.

Their lips were very shiny, and they smelled vaguely like cough drops.

"What craft did you guys do?" I asked them.

"We made natural lip gloss," Dana answered in a voice that made me feel like I should have known that without asking. But how could I have? I'd never heard of natural lip gloss. I was surprised Dana and Addie had heard of it, especially since I figured the Pops thought the only things worth having could be bought at the mall.

"Claire and Maya said some kids made it last year for their nature craft project, and it sounded perfect for the four of us," Addie told me. She rubbed a little on her lips. "Mmmm . . . It makes my lips so soft."

"How'd you make it?" I asked.

"It was easy. We just heated four ounces of sweet almond oil, two ounces of beeswax pearls, and a few drops of wheat germ oil. Then we added a little bit of camphor oil, which helps chapped lips. When it cooled, we put the lip gloss in the containers," Addie explained. "Of course there was a counselor there to help us."

"Can I try some?" I asked her.

The minute the words were out of my mouth, I regretted them. I don't know what made me ask Addie for a sample of her lip gloss. Maybe it was because she and I were finally having a civil conversation, and so I thought she might say yes. Or maybe it was just that it smelled so good. Either way, I hadn't expected her to go nuts on me.

"No, you can't," Addie told me flatly. "Just because we're sharing a cabin doesn't mean you can share my stuff. Dana and I were assigned to this cabin. We didn't choose to room with you. And even though you probably wish it would, nothing of ours — not even our lip gloss — is going to rub off on you!"

Yikes! I had no idea where that had come from. At least not at first. Then I noticed Maya and Claire walking up the steps of our cabin. They'd probably heard everything through the screen windows. Addie was showing off, making sure her Pop friends didn't think she'd been contaminated by being in the same cabin with a bunch of non-Pops like Sam, Chloe, and me.

Maya and Claire walked into the cabin and breezed right past Sam and me and over to Dana and Addie's side of the cabin.

"Are you about ready to go to lunch?" Maya asked.

"Just one more little bit of lip gloss," Dana said, wiping more of the clear gel onto her mouth.

"Mmm. Can't have too much," Addie added. She looked into her mirror, and shook her head. "This is the worst," she added. "I can't believe Mrs. Johnson took away the blow-dryer and the straightener."

Sam rolled her eyes. I knew exactly what she was thinking. She and Dana had blown out the power in three cabins. *Of course* Mrs. Johnson had taken the dryer and the straightener away.

I knew Addie couldn't be pleased with how she looked. Addie has really, really curly hair. Most of her hair looked fine — except for her bangs. The way they were cut, they had to be straightened flat in order to look good. But without a straightener, the bangs were kind of ballooning out to the side, like curly blobs on either side of her head.

"Just pin your bangs back," Claire suggested.

"I didn't bring any hair clips," Addie told her.

I had plenty of hair clips in my bag. But I didn't mention that to Addie. Not after what she'd just said to me. Besides, she never would have taken them from me in front of the other Pops, anyway.

"What's the afternoon activity?" Dana asked Maya and Claire.

"I'm not sure," Maya said. "Mr. Sabatino said they'd announce it at lunch."

"A mystery activity," I whispered to Sam. "Sounds like fun."

The Pops didn't seem to think so, though. As always, they looked bored. They looked at me, rolled their eyes, and walked out the door.

My friends, however, were anything but bored. We were all having a blast at Camp Einstein, and we didn't think it was uncool to show it.

"Do you think we're going to go on a hike again

this afternoon?" Liza asked as we sat around our lunch table.

"I doubt it," Marilyn answered her.

"There are too many of us to all go on a hike at once," Carolyn added.

"Maybe we're going to have relay races," I suggested. "We did that a lot at my camp last summer."

Marc shook his head. "That's regular camp. At science camp almost every activity has to be educational. There's nothing to learn from relay races."

"Sure there is," Josh argued. "You can study heart rate and muscle tone. That's biology."

Marc shrugged. "I guess."

"Maybe we'll have a scavenger hunt," Liza suggested. "We did that last year."

"That was so much fun," Marc added. "Do you guys remember what happened with Sabrina and Claire?"

Apparently my seventh grade friends did remember, because they all started laughing. In fact, they were giggling so hard, they couldn't get the words out to let the rest of us in on the joke.

"Come on, what's so funny?" Rachel asked them. "You know I always like a good laugh."

"Sabrina and Claire were in the woods, looking for some Queen Anne's lace," Marilyn began.

"And then they saw a spiderweb," Carolyn added.

"They totally freaked out," Marilyn continued.

"They were jumping around and screaming," Carolyn explained.

"And then Claire tripped over a log, and landed in this big mud puddle," the twins said together. Then they both started laughing again.

"And when Sabrina tried to pull Claire out of the mud, Claire fell again, and pulled Sabrina down into the mud with her," Liza explained between giggles. "You should have seen them. They looked like mud monsters."

"I wish I'd gotten a picture of that," Marc said.

"Well, if we're lucky, this year Claire and *Maya* will fall in the mud," Felicia said. "And hopefully, they'll take Dana and Addie with them."

"The Pops are being unusually obnoxious this week," Chloe pointed out. She looked over at Felicia and Rachel. "You two are lucky you're not sharing a cabin with any of them."

"I know," Felicia said. "It's got to be awful for you guys."

"It is," I agreed. "But luckily we never go to any of the same activities, so we barely see them. If everything goes well, I'll be able to avoid Addie and Dana pretty much all day."

Unfortunately, things don't always go the way you plan. I learned that the minute Mrs. Johnson stood up and walked to the center of the mess hall.

"May I have everyone's attention, please," Mrs.

Johnson shouted. "I'd like to tell you all about this afternoon's activity."

My friends and I quieted down immediately. We were eager to hear what we were going to be doing next.

"You're all going to do trust exercises," Mrs. Johnson told us. "You will each be given a partner," she said. "One partner will lead the other through a short hike in the woods. That's where the trust part comes in. The person who is being led will be blindfolded. He or she will have to trust that the seeing partner is able to lead them safely to the end of the trail. You will each get a chance to lead and to be led."

"Being blindfolded in the woods sounds pretty scary," I whispered to Chloe, who was seated beside me.

"Don't worry, I'll be your partner," Chloe whispered back. "You know you can trust me."

"True," I told her. And that did make me feel better.

But not for long. Because the next thing Mrs. Johnson said was, "The teachers and counselors have made a list of partners. It's posted on the back wall of the main office. You can see who you've been paired up with right after lunch."

"We don't get to pick our own partners?" Maya asked from her seat over at the Pops' table.

Mrs. Johnson shook her head. "That's part of the adventure. You have to learn to trust somebody you don't usually lean on."

"I guess we can't be partners," Marilyn and Carolyn said at once.

Sam laughed. "I'm pretty sure the teachers know you chum around together," she teased. "They're going to split you up for sure."

"I don't understand why we can't be with our friends," Chloe moaned. "It's like they want us to be miserable or something."

"I think they just want us to experience new things, and new people," Liza told her. "Besides, it's just one activity. It won't last long."

"I wonder how they picked the partners," Felicia said.

"Yeah, how do the teachers and counselors know who we're all friends with?" Rachel asked.

"Teachers pay attention to everything," Marc pointed out. "I mean you just have to look at this mess hall to see who's friends with who. It's not too hard to figure out."

"You guys don't think they'd pair us off with anyone we really couldn't stand, do you?" Chloe asked nervously.

"They could," Josh said. "Anything's possible."

I looked down at my plate of food. Suddenly I wasn't so hungry anymore.

"Come on, you have to look," Liza said as she pulled me toward the crowd of kids who were already gathered by the main office, checking out the trust exercise list.

"You don't know that you got one of the Pops as a partner."

"But I could have," I told her. "And as long as I don't look at the list, it hasn't happened yet."

"Interesting logic, Jenny," Liza said. "I wish Josh was here to tell you the seven million reasons that doesn't make sense, but he's back in his cabin getting his sweatshirt."

"Who'd Josh get as a partner?" I asked her.

"He said he got Ian Burns," Liza replied.

"Ian is nice. Josh got a really trustworthy partner," I told her.

"You might have gotten one, too," Liza said. "Come on, just look."

Slowly, I followed Liza up to the board. I ran my eyes down the list, searching for my name. Finally I spotted it. And there, in black and white, my worst nightmare came into view:

Jenny McAfee / Addie Wilson

"Oh, man," I groaned.

"I'm so sorry, Jenny," Liza said. "But remember, it's just one exercise."

"I can't trust Addie," I told Liza. "She'll probably lead me into quicksand or something."

"I don't think there's quicksand at Camp Einstein," Liza assured me. "And besides, you have to lead her around, too. She can't be too mean if she wants to be able to trust you when you lead her around."

Just then, Marilyn and Carolyn came running over. Marilyn looked happy, but Carolyn seemed miserable.

"I got Jessica as a partner," Liza told them.

"She's nice," Marilyn said. "I got Lee Ann. We worked together on a project in English once. I can trust her."

For once, Carolyn didn't finish her sister's thought. In fact, she didn't say anything. She just stood there, looking like she was about to cry.

"She got Claire as a partner," Marilyn explained to us.

"Oh," Liza replied. There wasn't much else she could say.

"Don't feel bad," I told Carolyn. "I got Addie."

"Addie's not as mean as Claire," Carolyn insisted.

"Claire is pretty much the meanest Pop," Marilyn added.

"Except for Sabrina, and she's not here," the twins finished in unison.

"The Pops are all mean," I told her. "Do you think if we asked to change partners, Mrs. Johnson would let us?"

Liza shook her head. "Teachers never let you do stuff like that."

I knew Liza was right. In fact, she'd just stated another one of those middle school rules you don't find in the official middle school handbook.

MIDDLE SCHOOL RULE #35:

TO TEACHERS, EVERYTHING IS AN IMPORTANT LEARNING EXPERIENCE. THAT'S WHY THEY WON'T GIVE YOU A PARTNER WHO IS YOUR FRIEND.

I sighed. Liza was right. And the last thing I wanted right now was to hear a lecture from a teacher. I was going to have to be Addie's partner. And I was going to have to trust her.

It wasn't going to be easy.

Chapter SIX

"OKAY, NOW TURN TO THE RIGHT," I said as I led Addie around a tree and through some low brush. "There's a bush to your left, and some grass straight ahead."

"Slow down, Jenny," Addie groaned as she walked. "Ooo, gross, what just went through my hair?"

"It's just some leaves from the tree overhead," I told her.

"It felt wet," Addie said.

"It was just some dew that didn't burn off of the leaves this morning," I assured her.

"It better be," Addie snapped. "Because if any bird poop lands on my head, Jenny McAfee, I swear I'll . . ."

"It was just damp leaves, Addie," I repeated.

"Why'd you lead me under leaves, anyway?" she demanded. "Are you trying to mess up my hair?"

I looked at Addie. Ever since I could remember, Addie's hair frizzed up when the air was really humid, and today was no exception. Thanks to the heat and the moisture in the air, her hair was frizzing up in every direction. It wasn't the tree that was causing Addie's bad hair day. But I didn't tell Addie that. We were already arguing with each other nonstop. Why make it worse?

"I'm just trying to get this activity over with as quickly as possible," I told her. "Now take two steps to your left, so you can avoid tripping on a tree stump."

Addie sighed heavily, and did as she was told. "I don't know why the teachers would put us together, anyway," she said. "I mean this could have been fun if we'd been allowed to actually pick our own partners."

I totally agreed with Addie. I looked ahead of me and spotted Josh and Ian. Josh was laughing at something his blindfolded partner had just said. It looked like they were having a good time. Josh was lucky to have a partner who wasn't his archenemy.

"We're almost at the end of the trail," I told Addie. "Just a few more twists and turns. Move a little farther to your left."

Addie turned and walked straight into a bush. "Ow, that scratched!" she exclaimed.

"You turned too far," I told her. "And it barely touched your leg. There's not a scratch on you. I promise."

"Yeah, well, give me better directions, will you?" Addie demanded. "Remember, I'm leading *you* back to camp."

That last sentence sounded especially snide to me. I had a feeling Addie was going to make the walk as difficult for me as she could. But before Addie could take another step, or make another complaint, there was a loud scream in the woods.

"Ow! Ow! I can't believe you did that!" A girl's high-pitched voice rang out through the trees.

"That's Claire!" Addie shouted. She ripped off her blindfold. "She sounds hurt. I've got to go help her."

I was about to tell Addie that we were supposed to stay with our partners for the whole trust exercise, but I stopped myself. I knew that if one of *my* friends had been crying out like that, I'd want to get to her as quickly as possible. Then I remembered that Carolyn was Claire's partner. Claire had sounded pretty angry. And when Claire got upset, she got mean. That meant there was a good chance Carolyn was going to need a friend nearby, too. Quickly, I turned and ran off in the same direction as Addie.

We found Claire lying on the ground near an old tree stump. She was on her side, clutching her right ankle. Carolyn was standing next to her, staring in disbelief.

"I can't believe you did that," Claire barked up. "You led me right into that stump. I'll bet you did that on purpose."

"I didn't, I swear," Carolyn told her. "I said turn right. You turned left."

"Oh, please. That's not how it happened at all," Claire insisted. "Don't you think I know my right from my left?"

"Of course," Carolyn told her. "But maybe with your blindfold on, you got confused."

Claire scowled and clutched her ankle tighter. "Owww," she cried out. "It hurts so bad!"

"I'll get help," I volunteered.

"Claire's *my* friend. I'll get the help," Addie insisted.

"Addie, don't leave me here with these two," Claire pleaded. "Let them get a teacher or something."

I didn't appreciate the way Claire was talking about Carolyn and me, but seeing as she was lying on the ground in pain, I didn't think it was the best time to confront her about that. Instead, I grabbed Carolyn by the arm and pulled her down the path. "Come on," I said. "Let's go find a teacher."

A few minutes later, Carolyn and I arrived with Mr. Sabatino and Jesse, one of the male counselors at Camp Einstein. Claire was still on the ground, but she was sitting up and the color had returned to her face. She looked like she felt a whole lot better.

At least she did until she spotted us. Then she clutched her ankle and began to moan. "It really hurts," she told the teacher and the counselor.

"Do you think you can stand on it?" Jesse asked her.

Claire shook her head. "No way. It hurts too much. Do you think it's broken?"

Mr. Sabatino smiled kindly at her. "You probably just twisted it. But just to be sure, we'll take a ride into the nearest town and have a doctor at the hospital take a look at it."

Claire opened her eyes wide. "H-h-hospital?" she stammered.

"Don't worry," Jesse told her. "One of the counselors will be with you the whole time."

"Can't Addie come, too?" Claire asked him. "I'd feel better with a friend there."

"Sure," Jesse told her.

Addie shot me a triumphant smile. I could tell she was feeling very important at the moment. This whole situation was filled with drama. Addie loved being in the middle of any kind of crisis.

"Now, come on. Wrap your arms around my neck," Jesse told Claire. "I'll carry you back to camp."

Claire did as she was told. Then, as Jesse began carrying her back down the trail, she turned and sneered at Carolyn. "I should have known I couldn't trust you," she told her.

If Claire had meant to make Carolyn feel bad about herself — and I'm certain that was exactly what she was doing — she'd definitely succeeded. A small tear was already rolling down my friend's cheek.

"Claire's right," Carolyn said. "I really can't be trusted."

"Of course you can," I told her. "Claire's a jerk. She probably fell on purpose just to get out of hiking. You know she hates bugs and dirt and stuff."

Carolyn shook her head. "No. I was supposed to get her down the trail safely. That was the whole point of this exercise. And I couldn't do it. Which proves I can't be trusted."

I sighed. I could see how bad Carolyn felt. I also knew it wasn't entirely her fault. I wished I could find a way to show her how trustworthy she was. And then it came to me. I knew exactly what to do. "Come with me," I said, taking her by the hand.

"Where are we going?"

"To the computer lab," I told her. "I'm going to prove to you that you can be trusted."

As soon as we got to the lab, I hurried over to one of the computers and called up middleschoolsurvival.com. Then I scanned the quiz list until I found exactly the one I wanted. "Okay, Carolyn," I told my friend. "Once you finish this quiz, I think you're going to feel much better!"

Can You Be Trusted?

The answers you give on this quiz will determine just how trustworthy you really are. The question is, when you give those answers, do you swear to tell the truth, the whole truth, and nothing but the truth? In other words, can you be trusted?

1. **True or false: When I'm caught in a bad situation, I always find it's easier to tell the truth and take my punishment. Lying gets so complicated.**

Carolyn stared at the screen for a minute. "Remember when Marilyn and I used to switch places in school to take each other's tests?"

I nodded. They'd done that a few times. And they'd always gotten caught.

"Well, whenever the teachers figured us out, it was a bad situation. But we never lied about what we'd done. We always admitted it," Carolyn told me. "So I guess my answer is true."

"True it is," I said as I clicked the mouse over the word *true*. The screen flashed a second and then the next question popped up.

2. True or false: I don't go back on a promise. If I say I'll do something, I will.

"This one's tougher," Carolyn admitted. "Because sometimes I make a promise to do something with a friend without asking my mom or dad if I can. And then I have to break the promise if they say no. So I guess my answer has to be false." She looked kind of bummed about having to say that.

"Don't worry, there are more questions," I assured her as I clicked on the word *false*. "Try this one."

3. True or false: I am a really good keeper of secrets. Tell me something in confidence, and my lips are sealed.

"That one is true!" Carolyn said happily. "I'm amazing at keeping secrets. There are things I don't even tell Marilyn."

Now, that made me really curious. I was dying to know what could be so secret Carolyn wouldn't even tell her twin sister. But, judging from her response to the question, I figured she wouldn't tell me. So I didn't bother asking. I just clicked on the word *true* and waited for the screen to switch to the next question.

4. True or false: I am more careful with things I've borrowed than with my own things.

"That's true," Carolyn told me. "Marilyn and I are both more careful with other people's things. I think it comes from being twins and sharing all the time. You learn how bad you feel when your twin ruins your favorite sweater or something, and so you don't want to do that to her or to anyone else."

"True it is," I said, clicking the mouse. "Here's the next question."

5. True or false: If my friends are in trouble, they know they can come to me. I'll always be there to help.

Carolyn grew quiet. "I guess that one's false," she said quietly.

"Why?" I asked her.

"I wasn't very helpful to Claire, was I?" Carolyn asked me. "She'd have been better off with a different partner."

"For one thing, you're not Claire's friend," I told her. "And for another, it's not your fault she turned in the exact opposite direction you told her to. I'm your friend, and I know I can trust you. You would never do anything to purposely hurt me, would you?"

"No," Carolyn said in a small voice.

"Exactly," I continued. "And you wouldn't do anything to hurt anyone else. You're someone we can all count on to give us good advice, and to keep our secrets. I wouldn't be having half as much fun in middle school if I didn't know you."

That was the truth. Carolyn and Marilyn always brought a smile to my face. Especially the way they acted when they were together, always finishing each other's sentences and thoughts.

"Okay, click *true*, then," Carolyn said.

I smiled as I clicked the mouse over the word *true*. A moment later a fresh image appeared on the screen.

You answered 9 True and 1 False.

What do your answers say about you?

Mostly True: You are a trustworthy person who obviously values honesty and loyalty. Your friends are lucky to have someone like you in their lives.

Mostly False: It's time to take a long, hard look in the mirror. Is that the face of someone you would trust? If others can't trust you, sooner or later you may find yourself all alone. Luckily, this is a problem that's easily solved. Just think about how you would want to be treated, and then treat your friends the same way.

I smiled triumphantly. "See?" I told Carolyn. "You *are* trustworthy. And nothing that happened with Claire will change that."

"I guess . . ." Carolyn said. But her voice trailed off, letting me know she still wasn't completely convinced.

"Come on. Who are you going to believe?" I asked her. "A Pop or a scientifically constructed quiz? And before you answer that, let me remind you that we are currently at a science camp!"

Carolyn sighed. "Well, when you put it that way, I sort of have to trust what middleschoolsurvival.com says."

I smiled at her. "Exactly my point."

Chapter
SEVEN

CLAIRE CAME BACK TO CAMP on crutches with a bandage around her ankle. Obviously she had a sprained ankle, but the way she was complaining, you would've thought her leg was broken in three places and she might never walk again.

"It was horrible," I overheard her telling Maya and Dana. "We had to sit there for hours, and then they twisted my ankle all over the place trying to get the right angle in the X-ray machine."

"How long are you going to be on crutches?" Maya asked her.

Claire shrugged. "I'm not really sure. They said it could be a day or two or a whole week. It all depends on how well I heal."

"So you're not going to be able to do the night hike tomorrow?" Dana wondered.

Claire shook her head. "And it's all Carolyn's fault!"

Considering how much the Pops hated being on hikes or in the woods, Claire should have been thanking Carolyn for getting her out of most of the activities at Camp Einstein. But I had a feeling that wasn't going to be what

Claire would do at all. Knowing Claire, she was going to make my friend's life miserable.

Sure enough, Claire began her Torture Carolyn campaign at dinner that night. As we all stood in the cafeteria line in the mess hall, Claire hobbled over on her crutches and gave Carolyn a dirty look. "I can't carry a tray," Claire announced. "And since this is all your fault, I think you should have to do it for me."

Carolyn didn't say a word. She just nodded and picked up a tray. Then she placed a plate of salad on the tray.

"No, not that one," Claire said in a haughty voice. "I like more tomatoes. Try the one near the back."

Carolyn reached over and grabbed a different salad.

"Now I want pasta. But not one with too much sauce," Claire continued.

Carolyn looked over the plates of pasta until she found what Claire had asked for. Then she put it on the tray and moved on down the line.

"Do you *believe* her?" Felicia asked us angrily. "She's turning Carolyn into her servant."

"Oh, I believe it," Sam answered. "And I suspect she's going to be quite the taskmaster for the rest of the week."

I nodded in agreement. I had no doubt Claire was going to keep up this helpless-girl-on-crutches thing for as long as she could. For one thing, being on crutches made her the center of attention. And for another, torturing one of my friends was an activity she enjoyed a whole lot more than rock climbing or going on hikes.

"Marilyn, are you okay?" Liza asked our friend.

Marilyn shrugged. "I just feel bad for my sister. Do you realize that after she brings Claire's tray to the table, Carolyn's got to go all the way to the end of the line to get her own food? We'll all be finished eating before she even sits down."

"No, we won't," I promised her. "We'll just eat really slowly."

"Scientists say it's healthier to do that, anyway," Josh added. "If you eat slower, your food mixes with your saliva better and breaks down into smaller pieces. Then your body can digest it better."

Chloe made a face. "Suddenly I'm not so hungry," she said.

I laughed. "Nobody said science was pretty, Chloe," I told her.

"Science can be pretty awful, actually," Chloe replied.

So was being at Claire's beck and call. That became even clearer when Carolyn finally sat down to eat her dinner. She'd barely dug into her pasta and salad when we all heard Claire calling her name from across the mess hall.

"Hey, Carolyn," she shouted out. "Can you get me another chocolate pudding? This is really good."

Carolyn stood up, but Sam stopped her. "Don't you dare! One of her friends can get the pudding for her."

I agreed with Sam. It would have been no big deal for Addie, Dana, or Maya to have gotten up and gotten a bowl of pudding for Claire. But none of them moved.

"Besides, she's already on her pudding, and you haven't even started your main course yet," Felicia pointed out.

Carolyn turned in Claire's direction. I could see her staring at Claire's bandaged ankle, and then glancing over at the crutches leaning against the wall. "I know. But the Pops aren't exactly volunteering. I'm the one who hurt her. That makes this my responsibility." She got up and headed toward where the bowls of pudding were set up.

"This is bad," Marilyn said with a sigh.

"Really bad," I agreed.

"Claire's going to ruin her whole week," Felicia added.

"Maybe not," Liza said, trying to sound optimistic. "It's just a game Claire's playing right now. She'll move on to something else really quickly. Pops have very short attention spans."

Not short enough. As the evening went on, Claire did her very best to make sure Carolyn did nothing but chores for her. She made Carolyn go back to her cabin to get her a sweater. Then when Carolyn came back with her purple sweater, Claire sent her back again to get her black one. It was absolutely ridiculous. But Carolyn felt so guilty she just couldn't say no.

Sam, on the other hand, had a *lot* to say about the way Claire was treating Carolyn. And a little later, after Carolyn was finally able to join us for the sing-along at the campfire, Sam made sure we all knew how she felt about it.

"Claire is a nasty grizzle," Sam announced, speaking loud enough so we could hear her over the singing campers.

"She's a what?" I asked.

"A grizzle. A whiner," Sam explained. "She just has a sprain! I broke my leg when I was seven and I was in a cast for six weeks. I didn't complain as much in six weeks as she has in one day."

I nodded in agreement. Claire was a jerk. But at least for the moment, she wasn't bothering Carolyn. We were all able to enjoy singing around the campfire together. Mr. Sabatino had just started to play one of my favorite campfire songs. I began to sing along. So did pretty much everybody else in the sixth and seventh grades. Except, of course, the Pops. I guess they thought singing around a campfire wasn't cool enough for them. How ridiculous is that?!

"If I had a hammer," I sang out, "I'd hammer in the mor-or-ning, I'd hammer in the evening . . ."

I could hear Sam and Chloe singing beside me. They really had incredible voices, and somehow, they were able to sing the song in perfect harmony — which was really funny when they began to make up their own words.

"If I had a hammer, I'd bop Claire in the head, head, head," they sang, just loud enough for my friends and me to hear them.

We all burst out laughing, which made everyone stare at us. They had no idea what was so funny about an old camp song.

As the song came to an end, Sam stood up and slid a marshmallow onto a long stick. "Enough singing. I'm in the mood for a sweet. I'm going to melt this one over the fire."

"Wait for me," Chloe said. "I'm going to set my marshmallow on fire. I love when they get all burned and black on the outside."

"Not me," Liza disagreed. "I like them browned evenly all around."

I smiled. Even Liza's marshmallows had to be a work of art.

"I think I'll make one, too," Carolyn said.

"Wait for me," Marilyn added.

"Marshmallows over a fire are the best," the twins finished their thought at once.

Felicia grinned. "It's good to hear you guys sounding like yourselves again. Claire's had Carolyn running around so much, I haven't heard that twin thing since this morning."

The twins shot Felicia a mirror-image smile. But their grins didn't last long. A moment later, Claire hobbled over to us. She stared at Carolyn. "Do you think you can stop talking to Mrs. Science Geek here long enough to roast me a few marshmallows?"

Felicia bristled at the name Mrs. Science Geek. "Why are you such a jerk?"

Claire shot Felicia a look and then completely ignored her. Instead, she turned her attention to Carolyn. "I'm the only one here who hasn't had any marshmallows yet."

"Not true," Marilyn said to her. "We haven't had any, either."

"Yeah, well, that's not my fault," Claire replied. "But my ankle is your sister's fault. Because of her, I can't stand near the fire and toast marshmallows."

"Why not?" I asked her.

Claire looked at me like I had three heads or something. "Because I need to keep my hands on my crutches. If I don't, I could lose my balance and fall into the fire."

I highly doubted that would happen. But before I could tell Claire she was being ridiculous, Carolyn stood up. "I'll toast you a marshmallow," she told Claire.

"I want two," Claire said. "And don't burn them. I hate it when they're burned."

As I watched Carolyn walk over and poke two marshmallows onto a stick, I knew that marshmallows weren't the only things feeling the heat tonight. The way Claire was treating Carolyn really burned me up!

By the time I got back to the cabin that night, I was exhausted. It was much earlier than I usually went to bed back at home, but somehow I was so much more tired than usual. Even the lumpy camp mattress felt good as I slid under the covers and shut my eyes.

But not long after shutting my eyes, I was awoken by the sound of leaves crunching outside the cabin.

"Somebody's out there," I whispered to Sam.

"Can't be. It was lights-out a half hour ago," she whispered back to me.

"I heard something," I insisted.

"It was probably just a raccoon," Sam told me.

"Would you two shut up?" Addie called over from her bed. "I'm exhausted."

I sighed heavily. Sam was probably right. It was probably just a raccoon or a . . .

THUD! Suddenly someone – or something – crashed right into the side of our cabin. Now everyone in the cabin was awake. Wide-awake. And scared.

"Do you think it's a bear?" Dana asked.

"I don't know," I said.

"Well, you should know. You're the one who went to camp before," Addie insisted.

"I didn't see any bears at my camp," I told her. "The counselors said they were in the woods and to keep food out of the cabins so the bears wouldn't come looking for it. So we did what they said, and we never saw any bears."

THUD.

"There it is again," Addie screamed. She hid her head under her blanket.

"Like that's going to help," Chloe said. "You can't hide from a bear."

"Or a monster," Dana added. "What if it's some kind of monster? Like the kinds you see in those horror movies."

"There are no such things as monsters," I told her.

"How do you know?" Dana asked me. "You've never even seen a *bear*!"

"Well, neither have you," I reminded her.

"Shhh . . ." Sam ordered. "Maybe if we're really quiet, it will go away."

That sounded pretty logical. So we all shut our mouths and sat there, staring into the darkness. And it worked. The noise outside stopped. There were no more crunching dry leaves or thuds against the wall of the cabin.

But there was a red light. A deep, bloodred light that had suddenly appeared, shining up through the window near Chloe's bed.

"AAAAAHHHHHHH!" Chloe, Sam, Dana, Addie, and I screamed as loud as we could.

"It *is* a monster!" Chloe cried out.

We all ran to the window. Sure enough, there was a red, creepy face staring up at us. I couldn't make out the hair, the nose, or the mouth. All I saw were eyes. Glowing red eyes.

"AAAAAHHH!!!!" We all ran to the far end of the bunk and huddled together.

"I told you there were monsters!" Dana shouted at me.

Leave it to Dana to insist on being right at a time like this.

Suddenly we heard giggling coming from outside the cabin.

"Hey, I know that laugh," Chloe said.

"So do I," Sam added.

I knew the sound of that laugh, too. I'd been hearing it since kindergarten. "Rachel!" I exclaimed. Then I ran to the door and peeked outside.

Sure enough, it was Rachel and Felicia. They were practically doubled over with laughter.

"It was you two!" I exclaimed.

Felicia was laughing too hard to do anything but nod. So Rachel did the talking. "You should have heard you guys. 'Aaaahhh! It's a monster!'" she said, imitating us before she broke into another round of laughs.

By now, everyone else in our cabin was outside with me. We didn't think the prank was nearly as funny as Rachel and Felicia did.

"All Felicia did was shine this flashlight right under my chin," Rachel told us, "and you guys were scared to death."

"I wasn't scared," Addie replied. "I knew it was just a stupid prank."

"Oh, right," Sam said. "That's why you stuck your head under your covers."

"Admit it," Felicia said, gasping between giggles. "We got you guys good."

"I won't admit it," Dana said. "We were just playing along because these three wimps were so freaked out. I wasn't scared at all."

I rolled my eyes. Dana had been the most scared of all of us. But I knew she would never admit it.

"You got us," Chloe told Felicia and Rachel.

But we weren't the only ones who'd been gotten. At just that minute, Mrs. Johnson appeared at our cabin.

"What are you girls doing outside?" the science teacher demanded.

"Um . . . we . . . um . . . we heard a noise," I said quickly. "So we came out to investigate."

"A noise?" Mrs. Johnson asked.

Sam, Chloe, and I nodded. But Addie just smiled triumphantly. "The noise was them," she said, pointing to Rachel and Felicia. "They were pranking us."

Mrs. Johnson looked at Rachel and Felicia. "Is this true?" she asked.

My friends nodded. "It was just a little joke," Rachel said.

"A joke?" Dana repeated. "It wasn't funny. You could have given one of us a heart attack by sneaking up on us like that."

"I thought you said you weren't scared," Chloe reminded her.

Dana rolled her eyes. "I said *could* have. They could have if we'd been scared."

"Well, girls," Mrs. Johnson said, looking directly at

Felicia and Rachel. "You broke the rules, and now you have to take your punishment."

Now it was Felicia and Rachel's turn to look scared.

"Tomorrow morning you two will have to get up early with the kitchen staff. Then you will serve breakfast to everyone else before you eat," Mrs. Johnson told them.

Rachel and Felicia looked miserable. And things were about to get worse.

"And don't worry," Mrs. Johnson continued. "I'll make sure they have extra hairnets and rubber gloves for you."

"We have to wear *hairnets*?" Felicia asked with a grimace.

"Oh, yes," Mrs. Johnson replied. "It's the law."

As I looked at Mrs. Johnson, I could swear I saw a little smile forming on her lips. Or maybe it was just the shadows. I don't think I'll ever know for sure.

Chapter
EIGHT

I FELT REALLY BAD for Rachel and Felicia the next morning. There they were, spooning oatmeal into bowls while the rest of us were happily chowing down and getting ready to start our next day at Camp Einstein. The Pops were in especially good moods.

"Lovin' the hairnet, Felicia," Dana said with a laugh. "It's totally you."

"Yeah, I hear it's what all the science geeks will be wearing this summer," Maya added. "Did you get a matching one for Josh?"

"Rachel can give him hers," Addie pointed out. "Unless it's all sweaty and gross. Which, from the look of her hair, I suspect it will be."

Felicia opened her mouth to say something, but the head chef shot her a look. Felicia sighed and plopped a bowl of oatmeal on Addie's tray.

The mess hall during breakfast was definitely different than it was during lunch and dinner. At the later meals, it was a noisy place, full of voices and laughing. But breakfast was much quieter. Nobody was particularly talkative in the morning, not even the counselors or the teachers, all of whom seemed to be spending an unusual amount of time near the coffeepots.

But Claire didn't seem to be at a loss for words. In fact, she was full of things to say. Or make that orders to bark — right at Carolyn.

"I need a bowl of oatmeal, Carolyn," Claire called across the room.

"I already got you a plate of pancakes," Carolyn called back.

"I didn't like them," Claire told her. "And I can't get the cereal myself. I can't carry a bowl and use my crutches at the same time."

Carolyn sighed heavily and stood up. "Fine," she responded.

"Oh, stop groaning," Claire told Carolyn. "I'm the one who should be complaining. I'm in so much pain."

She sure didn't look like someone who was in pain. In fact, there was a big grin of satisfaction plastered on her face. She was clearly enjoying herself. And so were the rest of the Pops. They were all snickering and giggling as Carolyn went up to get Claire's bowl of cereal. At least I *thought* Addie was giggling. It was hard to tell what she was doing behind the mound of hair that was blocking her face from my view. It had rained in the middle of the night, and now the humidity was even worse than it had been the day before. All that moisture seemed to have become trapped in Addie's ever-expanding curls. I have to admit I got a kick out of watching her hair get bigger and bigger with each passing moment.

"Night hike tonight," Marc reminded us as he smeared some butter on his stack of pancakes.

"Can we all go together?" I asked him.

Marc shook his head. "Seventh graders take a different path from the sixth graders."

"That stinks," Chloe complained. "We hardly get to do anything with you guys."

"If you think camp stinks for us, look at my sister," Marilyn said, pointing across the room. Carolyn was now off getting Claire a second carton of orange juice.

"How much do you want to bet that Claire's ankle miraculously improves after the night hike tonight?" Marilyn continued her own thought.

"You think she's faking?" Liza asked her.

"Oh, yeah," Marilyn said.

"It makes sense," Marc agreed. "You know the one thing she hates is hiking in the woods."

"She doesn't look like she's really in pain," Josh added. "She was barely leaning on those crutches when she came in this morning. It wasn't until she saw Carolyn that she really started hamming it up."

"But the hospital bandaged her ankle," I pointed out.

"They probably just did that because she was complaining about her ankle hurting," Chloe said. "If she was really injured, they probably would have sent her home."

I thought about that. Chloe was right. If Claire was still at camp with us, she couldn't have been hurt that badly. At my summer camp, a girl in one of the older cabins broke her arm and her parents picked her up and took her home the next day.

"I'm telling you, it's the hike," Marc continued. "She doesn't want a repeat of last year's spider incident. And nighttime is when all the creepy creatures come out."

"But what would she do here while we're all on our night hikes?" Rachel asked.

"Probably just skive around," Sam said.

I didn't exactly know what *skive* meant, but from Sam's tone I figured the definition wasn't "to work hard."

"Mrs. Johnson won't let her just hang out," Felicia insisted. "She'll probably make her do something else."

"Whatever that something else is, it won't involve any hiking, and that's what I think Claire's trying to be sure of," Marc said.

"Too bad we can't prove she's faking it," Rachel said.

"Who says we can't?" Chloe said.

I could tell by the grin on Chloe's face that she was hatching a plan. I didn't know what the plan was, but I was certain that the minute Chloe had it all figured out, she'd let us in on it. And I couldn't wait!

In the meantime, I was distracted from thinking about Chloe's plan by our morning activities. Marc, Rachel, Felicia, Josh, and I had all signed up for basketball. My friends and I play a lot of basketball at home because Marc has a hoop hanging over his garage door, so I figured the five of us were prepared for whatever any other team of five could throw at us.

If we'd been playing ball at summer camp, we would have just started the game immediately, with the center forward from each team having a jump ball. But because this was *science* camp, first we had to have a whole lesson on how exercise affects the various muscles of the human body, particularly the heart. It was pretty interesting, because they taught us how to take our heart rate by checking the pulse points in our wrists and necks. Josh, in particular, had a lot of questions for the counselor in charge. He seemed really into learning about heart rate and how exercise affects the blood flow to your muscles. I was glad there were no Pops around. There definitely would have been a few Mr. Science Geek references thrown around during the presentation if *they'd* been there.

But the Pops were off doing some other activity — probably something where they didn't have to get dirty or sweaty. Pops and camp are two things that just didn't seem to get along too well. I was glad, though, because that meant that Claire had signed up for something that kept her off her feet. Carolyn had been able to go sailing with her sister. From the basketball court, I could see the twins in their boat on the lake.

I didn't have time to think about the twins for very long, though. Once we were on the court, I was totally focused on getting the ball in the hoop, and keeping the other team from doing the same thing.

Our team won the game, 28–17. It was a total slaughter. I was feeling pretty good about myself until I walked into the cabin for a quick shower before lunch. That's when I ran right into Addie and Dana. They were sitting on Dana's bed. Next to them were two potted plants — obviously the result of their morning activity. Bo-ring. I could do gardening with my grandmother any time if I wanted to. Why waste valuable camp time doing it?

"Oh, gross," Dana said as I walked inside. She used two fingers to pinch her nose tight. "I could smell you before you got here. Of course, I thought it was a skunk. . . ."

Addie giggled. "Of course," she said, agreeing with Dana.

"Stay away from us, you sweaty skunk," Dana continued.

"I have to get past you to get to the bathroom," I told her. "I can't help it if you two got stuck with the beds right near the shower."

"Well, make it quick," Dana said. "And please use a lot of soap. I don't want that stinky sweat smell in the cabin for too long."

"I can't stand the Pops for another second!" I complained half an hour later as Chloe, Sam, and I joined Liza,

Marilyn, and Carolyn on some benches outside the mess hall before lunch.

"*You* can't?" Carolyn asked.

"Carolyn's had it worse than anyone," Marilyn reminded me.

"Claire can be such a pain," the twins said, finishing their thought together.

There was no arguing with that. Carolyn had had it pretty bad since Claire had sprained her ankle.

"Speaking of Claire . . ." Liza began. She looked over in the direction of the lake. Claire was just making her way up the hill with a few of the other Pops.

From what I could see, Claire was walking pretty well. In fact, she wasn't really using her crutches at all. She was just kind of dragging them along, happily walking beside her friends.

Until she spotted us, that is. Then suddenly she got a pained look on her face. She leaned on her crutches, and started hobbling across the grass.

"She *is* faking it!" I exclaimed. "Marc was right."

Carolyn's eyes shrunk to tiny, furious slits. Her face turned red. I had never seen her so angry. "I can't believe she isn't really hurt."

"Neither can I," Marilyn agreed.

But *I* could believe it. The Pops are capable of just about anything.

"Unfortunately, she'll never admit it," Liza said.

"She's got it too good this way," Carolyn agreed.

Chloe grinned. "Oh, she'll admit it," she insisted. "We're going to *make* her admit it. In front of everyone."

"How are we going to do that?" I asked. I was happy that Chloe was now going to reveal her plan. I'd been waiting all morning to hear it.

But Chloe wasn't giving us the details just yet. "You'll see when we get inside the mess hall," she told me.

"Why do we have to wait until we get in there?" I asked her.

"Because we want *everyone* to know what a faker she is," Chloe explained. She turned to Carolyn. "It's important that we take her by surprise. So you've got to act like you don't suspect a thing. Get her food, juice, water, whatever."

"Even though she's faking?" Carolyn and Marilyn asked together.

Chloe nodded. "It'll be worth it, I promise. Just you wait!"

There was nothing the rest of us could do but wait to see what Chloe's plan was — and if it would work. So that's what we did. We waited.

We waited while everyone got in line. We waited while Carolyn got Claire's grilled cheese and tomato soup. We waited while Claire hobbled over to the Pops' table and pretended to struggle to climb over the bench and then sit down beside Dana. We waited as Chloe got up to get a cookie, dragging me along with her.

"Just follow my lead," she told me.

"What lead?" I asked. But Chloe didn't reply. Instead, she started to scream.

"Eeeek! It's a mouse!" Chloe shouted. "Right there! Under Dana's feet."

Dana immediately leaped up. She jumped on top of the bench and started screaming.

At first, I wondered how making Dana jump on a bench was proving anything about Claire. But I caught on pretty quickly.

"I'll catch it," I said, diving under the Pops' table.

"Get it, get it!" Dana pleaded with me.

"Careful, Jenny, I think there's a spiderweb under the table, too!" Chloe shouted.

Now it was Claire's turn to freak out. "A spider?!" she shouted. She leaped to her feet and jumped up on the bench right next to Dana. "I hate spiders! I hate camp. Get me out of this place."

Chloe began to laugh. "Oops. I was wrong. That's not a spiderweb. It's just some dust."

Claire breathed a sigh of relief.

But not Dana. "What about the mouse?"

"Gone," I told her. "It must've run away."

"Thank goodness," Dana said. She climbed down from the bench and took her seat.

Claire started to climb down, too. But Chloe stopped her. "Boy, you sure are quick on your feet for someone with a sprained ankle," she said.

Claire stared at her. "What are you talking about?" she

asked. Then she suddenly realized what she had done. "I mean . . . um . . ." She grabbed her ankle. "Ow. It hurts again. I think I made the sprain worse or something."

"Nice try," Chloe told her. "Everyone saw you jump up onto that bench. And you weren't hurting a bit. You've been faking it."

"No, I haven't," Claire insisted feebly.

But it was no use. Everyone — even the teachers and the counselors— were onto her now.

"Claire, I'm so glad you'll be able to join us on the night hike," Debbie, one of the Camp Einstein science counselors, said. "It's always the highlight of the week."

I could feel Claire's furious eyes practically burning holes in our backs as Chloe and I walked away. But I didn't turn around. I just smiled triumphantly at my friends as I headed back to our table.

"I get the whole spider thing," I told Chloe as we walked. "But why scare Dana with the fake mouse?"

Chloe smiled happily. "That one was just for fun."

Chapter
NINE

"OKAY, ALL SIXTH GRADERS come with me," Mrs. Johnson called out that evening after dinner. "Our night hike will take the north trail. The seventh graders will be taking the eastern trail tonight."

I was kind of bummed that I wasn't going to be taking our last hike at Camp Einstein with Liza, Marc, and the twins, but I still had Chloe, Rachel, Sam, Felicia, and Josh with me on the trail. We all grouped together near the end of the pack of sixth graders, and awaited instructions on what to do next.

"Now remember, the whole point of this hike is to give you a sense of the world of excitement that goes on after dark," our science teacher told us. "We're going to try to experience all of it."

"Excitement. Yeah, right," Dana groaned. Then she yawned.

Josh shook his head. "Sometimes I just don't understand the Pops," he said.

"*Sometimes?*" Felicia asked him. "How about all the time? I never have any clue why they do the things they do."

"I just meant that a night hike is such a cool thing to do," Josh explained. "And it's really only something we'll get to do here. It's not like we can walk through completely dark woods at home. There are too many house lights and streetlights. And the park may have trees and grass, but it doesn't have any of the plant and wildlife we'll see tonight."

"Every group has been given a checklist. I want you to mark off each item on the list as a member of your group spots it," Mrs. Johnson continued.

Our group. I wish I could tell you that it was just my friends and I who were grouped together, but that wasn't the case. Each group had twelve people in it. And ours had Rachel, Felicia, Josh, Chloe, Sam, and me, as well as Josh's cabinmates, Michael, Zach, Andrew, and Evan. That would have been fine – if Mrs. Johnson hadn't put Addie and Dana in our group, too. I don't know why the teachers kept throwing them at us. There were other sixth graders at science camp, too. Shouldn't they have had to suffer through an evening of Addie and Dana? But we had no say in the matter. It was up to the teachers. And so we had to take to the trail with Addie and Dana in tow.

"Raise your hands if you have a compass," Mrs. Johnson called out.

Addie's hand shot up. She was the person in our group who had been chosen to carry the compass. Rachel was holding the clipboard with the checklist.

"Each of you should stick with your group. Do not separate from one another. The counselors and I will be interspersed among you, but should your group accidentally wander off the path, you can use your compass to help you return to camp. We'll be heading north on one trail until we see the waterfall," Mrs. Johnson said. "Then we'll take another trail south, heading back to camp."

"What if I get separated from my group and I'm all alone in the woods?" a girl named Cara asked. "I don't have the compass."

"I wish people would stop with the questions," Dana said, loud enough for Cara to hear. "The sooner we get started, the sooner we can finish this dumb thing."

"I doubt any of you will get lost," Mrs. Johnson assured Cara. "But if you do, the trees along the path heading north are all marked with white arrows. The trees along the path heading back to camp from the waterfall are marked with yellow arrows."

I sure hoped Mrs. Johnson was right about no one getting lost. I didn't want to have to depend on Addie to take me back to camp. I knew she hadn't paid close attention during the short lesson we had on using a compass. I don't know why the camp counselors had chosen to give her the compass. But then again, things like that happened to Addie all the time. She was usually the chosen one.

"All right, hikers," Mrs. Johnson called out. "Let's go."

And with that, we began our trek. The hike took us up a small hill, and then around the far side of the lake.

"Oh, check out those funny birds flying near the water," Rachel said, pointing up at some dark flying creatures in the sky.

"Those aren't birds," Josh told her. "They're bats."

"Very funny, Mr. Science Geek," Dana groaned. "Stop trying to scare us."

"I'm not trying to scare you. Those are bats. *Eptesicus fuscus* to be exact," Josh told her. "More commonly known as big brown bats."

"There's no place on the chart to check off bats," Rachel said.

"So just write it in," Chloe suggested. "Maybe we'll get extra credit."

"Maybe we'll get bitten and turn into vampires," Addie said. "Let's get out of here."

"That only happens in the movies," Josh assured Addie. "Big brown bats don't bother humans. They only eat insects and bugs."

"Well, you bug me," Dana told him. "So maybe you'll get eaten."

Michael and Zach giggled a little at that one. But Josh didn't seem to notice. He just kept walking, pointing out things along the trail. Nothing — not even Dana and Addie — were going to ruin his night. I was seriously impressed. I would have been really upset if someone had laughed at me like that.

"Okay, there goes a field mouse," Josh said, pointing to a little gray mouse that had scurried across a log a few feet away.

Dana gulped. Then she glared at Josh. "Was that a real mouse or another trick from one of you geeks?"

"It was real," Josh assured her. "But it's gone now."

"We still saw it, though," Felicia said. "So you can check it off, Rachel."

"Oh, cool!" Josh exclaimed suddenly. "Look up, you guys. I see the North Star."

"How do you know it's the North Star?" Felicia asked him.

"Because of where it falls in the Little Dipper," Josh explained.

"What's so great about the North Star?" Zach asked.

"For years, sailors used it to help them navigate," Josh explained. "If you're facing Polaris — that's the real name for the North Star — then you're facing north."

Dana yawned. "Bo-ring, Mr. Science Geek."

"I think it's really interesting," Felicia told her.

"That's why you're *Mrs.* Science Geek," Dana responded.

"That's getting really old, Dana," Chloe said.

"So is your shirt," Dana replied. "How many hand-me-down cycles has that T-shirt gone through?"

I looked over at Chloe. She didn't look upset at all. Then again, Chloe never cared what anyone thought of her clothes. If she liked something, she wore it. She didn't care if it was in fashion or not. And this shirt was classic Chloe. It had a picture of a sleeping dog on it, and it said, *I'm not lazy. I'm conserving energy.* I thought it was hilarious. I smiled at Chloe to let her know how cool I thought her shirt was. Chloe smiled back at me.

"Hey, you guys," Rachel said. "I think I hear something moving by that log. Maybe it's a raccoon. Let's go see."

"Do we have to?" Addie asked. "I'm tired."

"But we just got started," Josh insisted.

"I just want to sit on a log for one minute and rest," Addie told him. "Why don't you all go ahead? Dana and I will catch up."

"We're supposed to stick together as a group," I reminded Addie.

"Then I guess you're all waiting here for me, because I'm not moving," Addie declared. "My feet hurt."

And that was it. It didn't matter that the rest of us were eager to check off more things on our list (personally I was dying to spot an owl!), or that the rest of the groups were going to be way ahead of us on the trail if we stopped here. Addie Wilson wanted to rest. And so we were all going to rest.

Except Josh and Felicia, anyway. They were scouting around the area where we had stopped, looking for more things on our list.

"The fireflies are really out tonight," Felicia noted. "Check them off the list, okay, Rach?"

"Got it," Rachel said, placing a check next to the word.

"I can't believe how into this you guys are," Addie groaned. "So you saw a mouse and some fireflies. Big deal."

"Don't forget the bats," Evan said.

"Don't remind me," Dana countered.

"Come on, Addie," I urged. "We've got to keep going. The rest of the grade is way ahead of us now."

"Relax. We'll catch up. They didn't move off the trail or anything. How far can they be?"

Actually, they were pretty far away. They were at least far enough so we couldn't see or hear them anymore.

"I think you can add another animal to that list, Rachel," Sam said. "Is there a space for a sighting of a lazy sloth?"

"Who are you calling a sloth?" Addie demanded.

"You!" Sam shouted back. "Actually, you're lazier than a sloth!"

"You're such a jerk, Sam!" Addie barked.

"Ooh. Good comeback." Sam laughed sarcastically.

I was getting really sick of all the fighting. I could tell Sam was getting nervous about being so far from the rest of the sixth grade and all the counselors. And, for that matter, so was I.

"Can we just go?" I asked.

"Sure," Chloe said. "I'm sick of waiting for these two."

It seemed everyone else was, too. "Yeah, let's just go," Evan said.

"Seriously, dude," Michael echoed.

"We still have a lot of things on the list that we need to check off," Rachel informed us.

"That settles it," Chloe said triumphantly. "See ya later, Addie!"

"You guys can't just go," Addie said. "We have to stay together."

"It's ten of us and two of you," Josh told Addie.

"No wonder you're in advanced math," Dana replied snidely.

Josh rolled his eyes. "I'm just saying majority rules!"

Apparently, Josh was sticking to the mathematical rules about who was in charge, not the *middle school* rules. He wasn't intimidated by the Pops. That made me feel braver. So I joined the others and we began heading up the trail, leaving Addie and Dana behind.

"Hey!" Addie shouted. "You can't leave us out here alone. What if we get lost?"

"*You* have the compass," Sam reminded her.

But that didn't comfort Addie. She shot up from the log and hurried after us. I smiled happily to myself at the sight of Addie and Dana running along the trail to catch up to the rest of us. For once the majority really did rule! The Pops hadn't overruled us.

We followed along the trail silently for a while. I tried to focus on looking at the nature around us, searching for the things that were on our list. But my mind kept drifting off to the fact that no one from the sixth grade hike was in sight. It was like the twelve of us were all alone out there in the woods, and I was getting a little creeped out.

Things got worse when Chloe spotted an oak tree and Rachel checked it off the list. It wasn't the oak tree that was the problem. It was the fact that the oak tree was growing right smack in the middle of a fork in the trail.

"Which way do we go now?" Felicia asked.

"We have to follow the white arrows to go north, right?" Chloe mentioned.

I looked at the trees on either side of the fork.

"There are no white arrows," I said. "There are only blue or orange ones."

"That's not good," Josh said.

"Why not?" Evan asked him.

"Because it means somehow we ventured off the main trail," Josh explained.

"If we're not on the main trail, then where are we?" Addie asked nervously.

"I don't know," Josh told her.

"I thought you knew everything, Mr. Science Geek," Addie insisted.

"You're the one with the compass, Addie," he reminded her. "To get back to camp we have to go south. Which way is that?"

I could tell by the look in Addie's eyes that she had no clue how to read the compass. I also knew she wasn't going to admit it. Addie never admitted that she was anything less than perfect.

"Why don't you let Josh take a look at the compass?" I suggested.

"I'm not an idiot, Jenny," Addie shouted at me. She studied the needle on the compass for a minute, and then finally pointed behind her. "That way," she said. "That's the way we came from, right?"

"I'm not sure," Dana said. "We turned a little when we found the log to sit on."

"Yeah, but mostly we went straight," Evan pointed out.

"Okay, so let's go backward," Addie said, sounding a little more confident now. "That way we'll wind up back at camp."

Actually, that sounded logical to the rest of us, and so we followed Addie's lead back down the path.

"Ouch!" Addie exclaimed suddenly. She tripped over a log and fell on her face. Then she sat up and stared at Dana. "Why'd you push me?" she demanded.

"Sorry," Dana muttered. "You were going slower than I was. I just bumped into you."

"Well, don't do it again," Addie told her. "I could have banged my head on something and gotten seriously hurt." Addie sighed as she stood up and started down the path. Once again, we all followed her, going slower this time. No one wanted to bump into her and face the rage of Addie.

"I've never seen that group of pine trees before," Josh said as we passed by a clump of evergreens.

"Maybe you just didn't notice it," I suggested to him.

Josh shook his head. "No, I would have noticed it. Pinecones are on the list. I would have told Rachel to check them off."

"And he didn't," Rachel added. "But I'll check them off now."

"So we didn't walk past a bunch of pine trees before," Dana said with a shrug. "Big deal."

"It *is* a big deal," I told her. "A huge deal."

"Why?" Dana demanded.

"Because it means we're lost," I told her. The minute the words were out of my mouth, I could feel a heavy knot form in my stomach. Lost. In the woods. At night. This was not a good thing. Not a good thing at all.

Chapter
TEN

"ADDIE, CHECK THE COMPASS again," Zach suggested.

Addie reached into her pocket. "Oh, no," she murmured.

"What?" Rachel demanded.

"The compass. It must have fallen out of my pocket when I tripped." She turned to Dana. "This is all your fault."

"My fault?" Dana snapped. "How?"

"You bumped into me and made me fall," Addie replied. "That's when I lost the compass."

"Well, you're the one who couldn't read the compass in the first place," Dana reminded her.

Ordinarily, my friends and I would have liked watching two Pops argue with one another. But tonight we were all too scared to enjoy anything.

"Is anyone else getting a little chilly out here?" Rachel asked, wrapping her arms around herself nervously.

"Mm-hm," Sam murmured in agreement. She scratched at her leg. "And a little itchy, too. Do you think we could have walked through some poison ivy?"

Josh shook his head. "I didn't see any. Besides, I don't

think they'd let us go on a night hike in an area that was known to have poison ivy."

"*Known* to have," Chloe repeated. "But what if they didn't know it? I'm starting to itch, too."

"It's probably just mosquitoes," I said. "We got those a lot up at Camp Kendale."

Addie scowled. "Camp Kendale. Camp Kendale," she repeated. "You've been bragging about that place since you got on the bus to go there last summer."

"I have not," I told her.

"Sure you have. How about all those obnoxious letters you sent me? 'We went hiking to a waterfall. We made tie-dye shirts in arts and crafts. We went on a canoe trip and got to paddle through river rapids.'"

I stared at Addie in amazement. I had no idea she'd read any of my letters from camp. She'd certainly never answered any of them.

"And then on the first day of school, you wore that Camp Kendale T-shirt," Addie added.

"That thing with the lizard on it?" Dana recalled.

"It's the camp mascot," I explained weakly.

"Yeah, well, it was hideous," Dana said. "And so was the shirt. I bet Chloe wouldn't even have worn it!"

"Why would I wear a shirt from a camp I never went to?" Chloe asked her.

"That's not the point," Dana said. "The point is the shirt was so ugly even you wouldn't be caught in it."

"*That's* not the point, either," Addie corrected her. "The point is, Jenny was just wearing the shirt so she could brag about going away to camp while the rest of us stayed home."

I stared at her in amazement. I didn't know what to say. Was it possible that Addie had been jealous about me going to camp? Was that why she had ignored my letters? Was that why she'd dumped me?

It had never occurred to me that that was possible. After all, by the time I got home, Addie had already found her new group of impossibly popular kids, and she'd moved on. I'd figured that after she'd become a Pop, she thought I wasn't cool enough to hang out with her. It had never crossed my mind that Addie might be jealous of me — probably because I'd spent so much time being jealous of her since we'd started middle school. Addie Wilson. Jealous of me. Amazing.

Of course, Addie wasn't jealous of me anymore. Why should she be? I had only gone away to camp for seven weeks and three days. She was a Pop the rest of the year, which by my calculations was forty-four weeks and four days. Still, it did help me understand a little bit why Addie had so unceremoniously dumped me this year. And somehow, that made me dislike her a little less.

But not for long, because a minute later Addie was in my face, glaring at me. "Okay, Lizard Queen," she said.

"You're the big experienced camper. How about you get us back to camp?"

"I can't," I told her weakly. "This never happened at Camp Kendale."

"You never got separated from the group? Not even once?" Addie demanded. She sounded really angry that this had never happened before. And that made *me* angry.

"No, I didn't," I told her. "But then again, there was no one at my camp who was so lazy she had to sit down to rest fifteen minutes into the hike."

"I'm not lazy," Addie protested. "My feet just hurt. I have a blister."

"Maybe that's because you're wearing new, slip-on sneakers instead of hiking boots, which is what we're *supposed* to be wearing," I told her.

"Oh, so now you're the fashion expert?" Addie demanded.

"No, but I do know more about camping than you," I said.

"See, you *do* brag!" Addie shouted.

I stepped back and took a deep breath. This was getting ridiculous. Instead of fighting, we should have been working together to figure out a way to get out of the woods. That's when I remembered something Josh had said earlier that night.

"Josh, what was that you were saying about the North

Star earlier?" I asked him. "Didn't sailors use it for navigation?"

Josh nodded. "They said that if the star was in front of you, you were facing north."

"And aren't we supposed to be heading north on this hike?" I asked him.

Josh nodded. "But, Jenny, I don't know if it really works. It's just something I read about in a book. I've never really tried using the North Star as a guide before."

"Oh, great," Dana groaned. "What's the point of putting up with Mr. Science Geek all night if he can't even help us get out of the woods?"

I decided to ignore her. Fighting with Dana after fighting with Addie was just too exhausting. We all had to focus our energy on getting back to camp. "It's worth a try, isn't it?" I asked Josh.

"I guess so," Josh replied meekly. He looked up at the sky. "Okay, there's the Big Dipper. And right near it is the Little Dipper," he said, clearly speaking to himself. "And Polaris is . . . right there." He turned around so the North Star was in front of him. "This is north," he said, pointing ahead.

"So we want to go that way," Felicia said, pointing in the direction directly behind Josh. "South. Back to camp."

Josh smiled at her. "Exactly," he said.

Dana rolled her eyes. "Look, this is a lovely geek

moment and all, but I'd really like to get back to camp. So can we just move?"

And that's exactly what we did. We walked south. At first, nothing looked at all familiar. And then suddenly we began to spot things we had seen before.

"There's the oak tree!" Rachel exclaimed. "And the fork in the road where we made the wrong turn."

"Let's just make sure we take the right fork back to camp," I said.

"Actually, it's the *left* fork," Josh told me. "That's the one going south."

So we took the left fork. And we kept on walking, past the log where Addie first sat down, past the clearing where we'd spotted the field mouse, and along the lake where the bats were.

"I see lights!" Chloe shouted out suddenly. "Over there, just ahead!"

"We're back at camp!" Sam cheered happily.

"Josh! You did it!" Felicia exclaimed.

I smiled. She sounded so proud of him. Not that I blamed her. I was proud of Josh, too. And he wasn't even my boyfriend.

Boy, was Mrs. Johnson glad to see us when she got back to camp after the hike. "What happened?" she asked our group as soon as she spotted us near the campfire some of the counselors had set up.

"We made a wrong turn and wound up at a fork in the road," Chloe told her. "And we got lost."

"I'll bet you were glad you had your compass, weren't you?" the science teacher asked us. She looked at Addie in particular.

"Well, actually, um . . ." Addie began.

"The compass dropped out of Addie's pocket when she fell," Dana explained.

"You fell?" Mrs. Johnson asked Addie. "Are you okay?"

"Well, I have a blister on the back of my foot that really hurts . . ." Addie began.

Oh, no! I was not going to let Addie Wilson make this all about her. Not this time. It was Josh who deserved to be the center of attention tonight.

"Josh led us back to camp," I told Mrs. Johnson.

"He was amazing," Felicia added.

"It was no big deal," Josh said. "I just found the North Star. Once I knew where that was, it was easy to figure out which way to go."

"Well done," Mrs. Johnson complimented him.

"Hey, Josh, can you show me the North Star in the telescope?" Evan asked him.

"I was going to ask the same thing," Chloe said. "I figure I should know what to look for, just in case we get lost in the woods again."

A few minutes later, a whole group of sixth and seventh graders had gathered around the giant telescope. Somehow, word had spread about how Josh had led us back to camp safe and sound. He was kind of a hero. At least for tonight.

That's the thing about middle school. Nothing ever stays the same. One minute the Pops are the ones everyone wants to be around. Then suddenly everyone's dying to learn how to find the Little Dipper in the sky from Mr. Science Geek. You never know what's going to happen next. You just have to hope that sooner or later, everything will turn out okay. Just like it did tonight.

Of course, it helps to have amazing friends the way I do. If you have to be stuck in the woods, you want to be with friends who can make you laugh, like Rachel, and with friends who look out for you, like Chloe and Sam. And you probably would also want to be with friends like Felicia and Josh who are really smart and who can help you find your way back to camp again. When you have people like that in your life, you can pretty much survive anything middle school throws at you.

Grrr! Is This Girl Angry or What?

Anger can be triggered by all kinds of things — frustration, disagreement, or disappointment. The question is, how do you deal with anger-provoking situations? Are you a pouter, a shouter, a whiner, or a foot stamper? To find out your own personal temper tactic, take this quiz.

1. **You hinted for a month that you wanted an MP3 player for your birthday. Instead, your parents got you a sweater. What's your immediate reaction?**

   A. You walk around pouting all day long.
   B. Put on the sweater and pretend to be happy.
   C. Tell your mom that you're glad they didn't rush to get the MP3 player, because better models will be coming out soon.

2. **Your favorite movie star's new flick is opening tonight. You get to the multiplex forty-five minutes early so you can get the best seats in the house. Two minutes before the movie begins, a six-foot-tall man sits down right in front of you. How do you react?**

A. Ask him if he'll switch seats with you because you can't see.

B. Push your knees against the back of his chair so he'll become uncomfortable and hopefully move.

C. Sigh heavily and complain loudly to your friends that you can't see.

3. **You just found out that your sister took your favorite sweater without asking, and then tore a hole in it. What's your reaction?**

A. You scream at her and insist your parents ground her for stealing your stuff.

B. You ask her to replace the sweater as quickly as possible.

C. Forget about it. The sweater was getting kind of old, anyway.

4. **It's the championship basketball game. A player on the other team fouls you on purpose, and the ref doesn't see it. What do you do?**

A. Tell her you know what she's done, and next time you're going to make sure everyone else, including the ref, does, too.

B. Ignore it. She's just trying to psych you out. Why give her the satisfaction?

C. Have a fit, and tell the ref he needs glasses!

5. **You're supposed to go ice-skating with your BFF on Friday night. But at the last minute, she calls and tells you her aunt came into town and she's stuck at home with the family. What's your reaction?**

A. Tell her it's cool. Everyone has family obligations from time to time. Besides, there's a good show on TV you wanted to watch.

B. Inform her that you will never make plans with her again, then slam down the phone.

C. Sigh heavily, just to let her know that you're bummed.

6. **You're on a girls' night out at the movies. But when you get to the theater, you spot your boyfriend in the popcorn line with some girl you don't know. What do you do?**

A. Ignore it. There's probably a perfectly good explanation — maybe she's his cousin or something. Why let this ruin your girls' night?

B. Walk over and suggest he and his gal pal sit with you and your friends. Then watch him squirm as he tries to get out of it.

C. Walk up to him and ask him if he wants to share your popcorn — and then dump the whole bucket on his head.

7. You've been working on a clay sculpture project for art class for a week now. When you finally finish it, you leave it on the counter to dry. Unfortunately, your dog knocks the sculpture over and cracks it in two. How do you react?

A. You moan, groan, complain, and then try to glue the pieces back together.

B. You pull out some more clay and start over.

C. Call Fido a bad dog, and then retaliate by throwing out his favorite bone.

8. Your school art club has been planning its outdoor crafts fair for weeks now. But when you wake up on the morning of the fair, it's pouring rain. How do you react?

A. Storm around the house banging drawers and kicking doors.

B. Start to cry. It feels like bad things always happen to you.

C. Suggest that the club hold the crafts fair in the school gym instead.

Total Up Your Temper Tally!

1. A) 3	B) 1	C) 2
2. A) 1	B) 3	C) 2
3. A) 3	B) 2	C) 1
4. A) 2	B) 1	C) 3
5. A) 1	B) 3	C) 2
6. A) 1	B) 2	C) 3
7. A) 2	B) 1	C) 3
8. A) 3	B) 2	C) 1

What Does Your Score Say About You?

20–24 points: Ease up, firecracker! It doesn't take much to set you off. A temper like that can get you in big trouble if you're not careful. Try taking a deep breath instead of blowing smoke next time you feel yourself getting upset. Sometimes the things that make us angry are easily fixed if you just take the time to come up with a solution.

14-19 points: Congrats! You have control over your emotions, at least most of the time. You don't let a lot of things get you angry, but you do let others know when they've hurt or disappointed you.

8-13 points: You definitely know how to go with the flow. It's almost superhuman the way you stay serene through everything. But keeping your feelings all bottled up isn't always the best thing to do. It's okay to get upset once in a while. After all, you're a member of the human race. Emoting is what we do.

Here's a sneak peek at Jenny's next middle school adventure!

"Our student council yearbook photo session is next Friday," Sandee Wind, the eighth grade class president, announced. "Now, does anybody have any new business before we start planning the winter formal?"

I looked around the table. Everyone looked a little bored. Everyone but Addie and me, that is. As the sixth grade representatives, we were excited about planning our first formal dance. But none of the seventh or eighth graders seemed to think it was a big deal.

"What's there to plan?" John Benson, the eighth grade vice president, asked Sandee. "It's going to be exactly the same as last year's winter formal. And the one the year before that."

Now I was getting kind of bummed out. Ever since I'd heard about the winter formal, I'd been imagining a magical night, with everyone all dressed up, dancing under shimmering wintry decorations and drinking hot cider, while some really cool band played hit songs. You know, like you see in the movies or on TV.

But apparently that wasn't what the winter formal was like at our school.

"I guess we could hire Mr. Wilke to do the DJ stuff again," Kia Samson, the seventh grade class president, said with a sigh.

"But he plays classic rock," Sandee reminded her. "I don't think anyone wants to dance to eighties music. Yuck. My *parents* danced to that stuff."

"Well, who else can we get to do it?" Kia asked Sandee.

"Do we have to have a DJ?" I asked. "Wouldn't a band be more fun?"

Sandee nodded. "It would." She turned to Addie. "That band you got us from the high school for the first dance of the year was great," she said.

Addie sat up proudly and smiled. "Thanks," she said. "They played as a personal favor to me."

I rolled my eyes. That was such an Addie thing to say. Not that I could argue with her. It was exactly what had happened. Addie had definitely saved that dance by bringing in live music.

"Do you think they'd do it again?" Sandee asked her.

"No," Addie said, slumping back down in her chair like a deflated balloon. "Their bass player flunked geometry and he's grounded. No more gigs until he gets his grades up."

"That's the problem with a high school band," I said. "It's too bad we can't get someone professional in here. Someone who is really talented, but doesn't have to ask permission to play a gig at our school."

Sandee nodded. "That would be great," she agreed. "But who knows anyone like that?"

"Seriously, Jenny," Addie said with a sarcastic laugh. "Where would a bunch of middle school kids meet a talented, professional musician?"

I frowned. Addie never passed up a chance to make it seem as though my ideas were idiotic, especially at student council meetings. She was still angry that I'd been voted sixth grade class president and she was only vice president. So she made it her business to show me up whenever she could. If only I knew someone who knew someone who was a professional musician . . .

Suddenly it came to me. A solution so simple, I was surprised Addie hadn't volunteered it herself. Especially since *she* was the someone who knew someone who knew a musician!

"Why don't you ask your dad to ask Cody Tucker if he would play at our dance?" I suggested to Addie.

Everyone in the room leaped to attention at that. No one looked bored anymore. Everyone seemed thrilled and amazed. Everyone but Addie, that is.

"What are you talking about, Jenny?" she asked me nervously.

"Your dad works for the company that sponsors Cody's tour, right?" I asked her excitedly.

"Well, yeah, but . . ." Addie started.

"And you said your dad knew him, right?" I continued. "I heard you telling Dana about it in gym class."

"Why were you eavesdropping on our conversation?" Addie demanded.

"I wasn't," I said. "I was just standing right near you when you were talking."

"Well, then you heard me tell Dana it was a secret," Addie told me.

Suddenly I felt really uncomfortable. I hadn't meant to tell Addie's secret. But she'd been talking so loudly, I figured the other people in our gym class knew it, too. "I figured you'd bring it up anyway, as soon as you thought of it," I told her. "I mean you're the one who always does everything to make the dances great." I added that last part to make her feel good — and to make her stop shooting daggers at me with her eyes.

"Is it true, Addie?" Kia asked her. "Does your dad really know Cody Tucker?"

"Um . . . yeah," Addie said nervously. "But I don't think . . ."

"Addie, if you could get Cody Tucker to sing even one song at our school dance, you would be a legend!" Sandee exclaimed. "Our school would be written up in the newspapers."

"We might even get some TV news shows to come and film our dance," I said.

"It would definitely make this winter formal different from all the others," Ethan added.

"Well, I guess I could ask my dad to find out if Cody Tucker could sing just one song," Addie said. "But I can't promise anything. I mean, Cody's a busy guy."

"I know," Sandee told her. "And if he can't do it, we'll understand."

"I'm just excited to know someone who knows Cody Tucker," Kia said with a sigh. "Addie, you're so lucky."

Addie smiled at her. "I know. Did you see the shirt I was wearing yesterday? That's from Cody's tour. They're not even on sale yet. But my dad was able to get it for me."

From that moment on, there was no new business at our student council meeting. All anyone was talking about was Cody Tucker — even the boys. And Addie was just where she loved to be, at the center of it all.

Will Jenny survive middle school? Read these books to find out!

#1 Can You Get an F in Lunch?
Jenny's best friend, Addie, dumps her on the first day of middle school.

#2 Madame President
Jenny and Addie both run for class president. Who will win?

#3 I Heard a Rumor
The school gossip columnist is revealing everyone's secrets!

#4 The New Girl
There's a new girl in school! Will she be a Pop or not?

#5 Cheat Sheet
Could one of Jenny's friends be a cheater?

#6 P.S. I Really Like You
Jenny has a secret admirer!
Who could it be?

#7 Who's Got Spirit?
It's Spirit Week!
Who has the most school pride —
Jenny's friends, or the Pops?

#8 It's All Downhill From Here
Jenny has to spend her snow day
with her ex-BFF, Addie!

#9 Caught in the Web
Jenny and her friends
start a webcast, and so do
the Pops! Which show will
have more viewers?

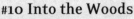

#10 Into the Woods
The sixth grade goes to science camp
and Jenny, Sam, and Chloe have to
share a cabin with the Pops!

Log on to my favorite website!
www.middleschoolsurvival.com

You'll find:
- Cool Polls and Quizzes
- Tips and Advice
- Message Boards
- And Everything Else You Need to Survive Middle School!